Ghosts on Ratchet Mountain

Deb Kemper

Charlie Dawg

Press

Deb Kemper

This book is a work of fiction. Any resemblance of the characters to real people is unintentional.

ISBN:

978-1944979-18-8

Prologue

Blue Ridge Mountains of North Georgia
March 1973

"Merlene, don't keep raggin' me over the damn muffler. It's supposed be loud. This here's a hotrod." Earl shifted into second gear and maneuvered cautiously along the narrow two-lane highway. Wipers slapped a steady beat, attempting to clear the windshield. As the altitude rose, rain pelted the car with sleet. Headlights reflected, instead of cutting a path through dense fog.

His tipsy wife screeched over the rough noise of the expensive upgraded exhaust. "I hate the way it roars! It makes my head hurt!" She stuffed her fingers in her ears.

Earl pulled to the narrow shoulder and parked The Beast, as he'd aptly named the recently rebuilt two door red-orange 1961 Chevy Impala SS.

He rubbed his dry, achy eyes and sighed, switched off the ignition and hooked his right arm behind his wife's seat. "Look, hon, we won't take it out again. From now on, when we go out together, we'll drive the truck." Peeved because she wouldn't look at him, he reached around and turned her face toward his. "I promise." His big cowy eyes usually got the better of Merlene.

1

Drunk and unreasonable, she jerked away, opened the door and, after checking for a foothold, vaulted from the low seat. "Screw you, I'll walk home!" She slammed the door hard enough to feel the impact in the heavy car.

Her tantrum kicked Earl's hangover headache into full throttle. He sighed, considered following her on foot, then mumbled, "Well, little lady we'll just see how much you hate it when you have to hear it with ever' damn step you take!"

When the machine roared to life she glanced behind, arms aloft for balance. Fearfully she watched her husband pull onto the highway, gunning the engine. She ran, but made only a few yards when her heels slipped on the wet road and her right ankle gave way. She fell to her knees, grimacing with pain, and screamed. The Beast's front bumper halted inches away from her forehead. She quivered from the adrenalin rush, colliding with the large amount of alcohol she'd consumed at Jimmy's Saloon.

The headlights blinded her.

Earl shouted, as he left the comfort of the car, to round the front. "Happy anniversary, bitch! You did your best to ruin the evenin' I planned and you finally topped last year's celebration. I'd tip my hat to you if I's wearin' one!" He hovered over his wife's upturned face, rain running down his collar. She spilt tears, because that's what always worked on Earl's heart. "Nah, no need to be cryin'. I've had it with your crap. Get your ass *up* and in the car."

Merlene whined and sobbed her way onto her feet, grabbing the bumper to pull her hefty weight from the ground. She stood for a moment to get her bearings before Earl grabbed her upper arm and urged her hesitant bulk forward.

"Get in and shut the hell up!" He pushed her the last few steps, which sent her tumbling. She twisted her ankle again.

She bawled and hugged the warm asphalt beside the loud car, but finally got to her feet to find her husband watching, hands on his narrow hips.

He growled. "Get in!"

She obeyed.

He pulled his door shut and reached across her lap to close hers. He gunned the engine and rolled his eyes her way. "You gotta lot o' makin' up to do tonight, Merlene Carson. Do you hear me?" He raced the engine again, his foot on the clutch, and put the car in gear to lurch forward, stirring the pea soup atmosphere.

Her hand gripped his crotch. "If you want me to, I can start now." She sniffed and wiped the runny mascara off her cheek.

He found a wider section on the shoulder and parked. He unzipped his trousers and turned the heater up full blast to shake the chill of his rain-soaked clothes. "Well, be at it then."

Maybe he's asleep, Merlene pushed herself upright, wiping her mouth, on her sleeve and studied her husband in the dim console lights. He faced the window. *Thank goodness! I could use a nap myself.*

The car idled loudly, but she was too tired to fight the lethargy. Besides, if she'd turned it off, she'd be cold again.

She leaned back, into the leather seat, closed her eyes and slipped away.

***

Patrolman Hoss Infinger parked in front of the Carson's car. He used caution approaching, one hand on his sidearm, eyes scanning the area. As far as he could see there was no one else in sight. The fog brightened with dawn, but the sun hadn't appeared to burn off the cloud cover.

He returned to his patrol car to call his report into the office. "May be another carbon monoxide poisonin'."

Leaving his car, with a hammer from his glovebox, he tapped the driver's window until it gave way, spilling inside and onto the blacktop.

He unlocked and opened the door, surveying the scene for a moment, then hurried to notify the dispatcher. "Yep, pretty sure that's what's happened. I saw both of 'em at Jimmy's last night. Call Earl's mama and get somebody over to the house. Them young'uns are prob'ly on their own. I'll wait here for Doc Henderson. Over and out."

Jeremiah Henderson parked his '72 Buick LeSabre behind Deputy Infinger's Ford. Hoss watched the doctor climb out of the comfort of his fine mint green coupe into the misty cold morning of the Blue Ridge Mountains.

"Hoss." Dr. Henderson nodded affirmation. "Wha' we got here, son?"

"Earl and Merlene Carson—both deceased." At nineteen, Hoss felt like he looked, a red-haired pimply-faced teenager beside the distinguished, graying physician. "Appears to be another carbon monoxide poisonin', sir."

Henderson frowned. "Good Gawd! That's eight in six months! That's epidemic damned proportions—" He looked up. "Sorry, Hoss, it's been a long night." He pulled on rubber gloves and leaned into the car to examine Earl Carson's slack cheeks and tilted his face up. "Lips bright red, chalky white skin, yep, seems you're right." He straightened, mumbling, "Sweet Jesus! What's gonna happen to their six children?"

He raked his fist across his dark scruffy cheek, sighed and studied the low clouds shrouding the pines and boulders above them. "Hoss, call in the ambulance to pick up the bodies for the morgue, then have the car towed in. I want Henry under that damn thing before noon. Let's see what it is this time. This has *gotta stop*." His black leather bag swung from his fingertips. "I'll be back at the hospital in a bit. Been up all night deliverin' babies. Need a nap." He wearily climbed into the LeSabre and pulled out around the two cars, heading home to his invalid wife and the nurse, whom he hired to live with them a year earlier.

A few moments of cold sunshine failed to burn away the clouds, as Jeremiah continued up Ratchet Mountain. He crept along at twenty miles an hour, his eyes widened. He hummed to stay awake. He relaxed when he spotted reflectors marking his driveway. He steered down the closely shaded, narrow road and stopped in the carport at one end of the stone house. He stretched when he stepped out, looking forward to a hot shower and a decent nap.

Jeremiah's housekeeper, Tabby O'Hern, opened the door, before he reached for the knob. "Herself ain't taken her medicine yet. Says she's waitin' fer ye." She propped her hands on her wide hips and swung her gaze toward the rear hallway with a grimace.

He handed over his black leather bag, hat and trench coat, then headed to his wife's bedroom, with a weary sigh.

Moaning from the pain of terminal ovarian cancer, Marcia attempted to push herself up to a sitting position, in the bed as he entered.

Jeremiah hurried to her side. "Hey, don't struggle." He softly touched her shoulders and propped her with pillows. "How's that?"

Her body quivered. His wife's swollen eyes met his. "I just wanted to see you for a moment before you left for work."

"I've been at the hospital all night. Louise had twin girls and Mary Ann Jacobs delivered a fine, plump boy." He wouldn't bring up the Carson's demise. The subject of death was too distressing.

She bobbed her head and raked her fingers through her thin dark hair. "Alright. I need to tell you—" She panted from exertion.

He steeled himself for the daily concern that today was the last day she had to live. "Yes?"

"I've forgotten." She rolled her dark blue eyes and exhaled noisily.

From the shadows of the room a shape emerged. Nurse Hill gently reminded her mistress, "You wanted to know if he'd take you for a drive on Sunday."

Marcia's eyes went blank for a moment. "That was it. So, will you?"

Her husband patted her hand, resting on the fold of the quilt covering her. "Of course, I will." He smiled and covered her fingers.

She watched his hand over hers and didn't move until he pulled away. He frequently forgot that his lightest touch was painful to her.

"Now will you take your medication?" He smiled congenially.

Without waiting for an answer, Nurse Hill filled a syringe, holding it up to the dim light of the window.

Marcia studied her savior, the precious morphine that gave her ease, and nodded mutely.

"Well, then, I'm off for a shower and a nap. I'll check in on you before I leave again." Jeremiah turned and rubbed his fingers together. Her skin felt clammy. Her kidneys had begun to fail.

7

Chapter One

Jeremiah glanced over the report the mechanic scribed on Earl Carson's Impala. He frowned and studied sunlight filtering through half-open blinds, in his office. He leaned back in the leather chair locking his hands behind his head and exhaled. *Leaky manifold again, gasket perforated in three places.* This time he'd find out who was responsible for the custom work on Earl Carson's vehicle. The gasket shouldn't have failed on a new installation.

He pushed away from his desk and snagged his brown fedora from the coat rack. His long legs carried him down the corridor and two flights of stairs to the lobby of the hospital. He slipped on sunglasses to guard his sensitive hazel eyes and made haste for the mechanic's shop, just a mile's walk.

Several patients greeted him along the way. He tipped his hat to Junal, June Allison Finley, a lovely young woman with a stunning smile. He couldn't resist a glance behind to watch her sashay toward her job at Lee, Compton and McDade, Attorneys at Law. Her red patent leather heels clicked along the concrete path. The skirt of the suit she wore fit across her perfect bottom smoothly. She stopped, turned and looked his direction with a smile on her glossy red lipsticked mouth, a dimple appearing in her right cheek and her short platinum hair lifting slightly with the breeze. Jeremiah had carried a torch for that gal since they were kids. He blushed and spun toward his objective.

A wave of nostalgia swept over him for the loss of his wife's youth and beauty. He nearly collided with Mack Ingram, the vicar from Ratchet Mountain Episcopal Church. "Beg y' pardon, sir." His mumbled apology was returned.

The vicar smiled and patted the doctor's shoulder, before moving on.

The sign above the metal Quonset garage read; *Henry Phipps, Mechanic Extraordinaire*. The noise of a revving engine drowned out the Athens radio station playing country music.

Henry yelled at someone in the car, "Turn it off!" He wiped his hands on a blue rag.

The racket died. A comely woman in slim-fitting jeans stepped out the open door. "So, what d'ya think it is?"

Henry scanned her. "You've blown a piston, darlin'." He beamed a perfect smile.

She crossed her arms, pushing her cleavage higher in her low-cut sweater. "Only in your dreams am I your darlin', Henry."

Jeremiah let his presence be known by clearing his throat.

Henry held his right arm up, to shield his eyes from the sun breaking through the trees. "Oh, hey, Doc, how are you?"

9

"Fine, Henry. Shall I wait in the office for you to finish with your customer?" He dropped his head and looked over his sunglasses, lips pursed.

Henry shook off the sarcasm. "Nah, we're done." He snatched a set of keys off a peg board and handed them to the young lady. "Here, Trix, you can drive my truck 'til I get it fixed."

Trixie beamed. "Well, alright then. I'll take you up on that." She plucked the keys from his fingers and set off toward his shiny red Ford truck around the corner.

Henry called after her, "Maybe someday you'll leave that sorry s.o.b. you're supportin' and want a real man who'd take care of you." He continued to clean his fingernails with the rag.

She blushed and nodded, her voice softened. "Thank you."

Henry watched her go, assured he'd planted seeds of doubt. He dragged his gaze to the intruder. "So, what can I do for you, sir?" He pivoted, heading to the office where a heater hummed in the corner.

"I read the report you made on Earl Carson's manifold gasket being broken in three places?"

Henry leaned against the wooden desk at the rear of the glass fronted room. "Yep, that's what I found."

"How could that happen on a newly installed manifold?" The doctor pushed his hands into his pants pockets, clearly out of his depth.

"Sloppy installer, dryrotted gasket, or it could have been done intentionally." Henry dipped his head and let his pale gray eyes rest on the car beyond Jeremiah's shoulder. "There's a fella down in Athens does a lot of those fancy mufflers. I heard tell, some time ago that he builds them himself. Could be Earl ran into the city to get the work done. I don't handle that sorta thing. I'm too busy as it is."

Jeremiah straightened. "I can see that. Did you look over the vehicles in the other cases of carbon monoxide poisoning?"

Henry sighed and rolled his eyes heavenward. "The last two I did. Nobody said anything about the first one, that I heard. You performed the autopsies?"

Jeremiah nodded. "I did."

"You have to understand there can be more than one way to make the exhaust leak into the car. I can think of ten right off and I'm not a psychopath." He grinned.

"I'll pull the files and take a look at them again. Give me the name of the muffler builder in Athens, please."

Henry pulled a stub of a pencil from behind his ear and scribbled a name on a receipt, tearing it off the pad. "I think it was Ned Turner who told me about 'im. If you run across 'im you might ask. He did business with the fella. And he's still breathin'."

"Thanks, Henry, I'll do that." The doctor stepped out into the chilled spring sunshine.

***

Jeremiah rubbed his eyes and stretched. Four hours passed while he went through the paperwork of all three of the proven carbon monoxide cases. The three cars were in various states of disrepair. Earl Carson's was the only one recently muffled. The deputy who handled the previous cases was the newly elected sheriff, Jackson Little.

The doctor sighed. Could it be anybody but that jackass?

His secretary, Mary Ellen Clark stuck her graying blonde head in the door. "I'm fixin' to leave. Do you need something before I go?"

He shook his head. "Think I'm alright."

She paused to study her boss.

"What?" The doctor's voice sounded harried.

"Just thinkin' how much you're like your daddy." Mary Ellen smiled. "Don't work so hard, it'll all be there tomorrow. Oh, and Sheriff Little came by earlier today. Wanted to know why you pulled the files on those old poisoning cases. Told him you *had* to have a reason. Maybe because you just autopsied two more like the others."

"Mmm." Jeremiah pondered the folder.

"I'll leave you to it, then." She closed the door and left for the day.

The general practitioner gathered the files neatly and stacked them on a corner of his desk. He wasn't ready for the stress of home. He decided to take a drive up the mountain to see about the Carson's children and parents and find out about final arrangements.

Chapter Two

The engine purred, as the Buick snugged into the curves of the mountain road. Jeremiah enjoyed the silence of the ride, bracing himself for the heartbreak of the family he was visiting. He drove past his own abode, where he was raised by his parents in the house his grandparents built when his father was a child.

He inherited the mountain shanty, as Marcia called it, from his parents. She disliked their home and the small town he served. She'd thought there would be more adventure in the Appalachian Mountains. Lack of local skiing and resorts were her favorite disappointment.

He brought her home to meet his parents once, before his father died. His mother moved to Atlanta as soon as he accepted the position offered by Highland Memorial Hospital. He and Marcia left Telluride, Colorado, after one short year on staff, in a large hospital, for the small town of Delilah, Georgia. The hamlet lay at the edge of the state line with South Carolina. The pampered daughter of a California real estate tycoon was quickly and easily bored.

Jeremiah slowly approached the Carson's long log house. The front porch ran the length of the place, at least 50 feet. The kitchen door stood open, screen closed until a tow-haired boy of about four dashed through, a beagle pup on his heels. The slap of wood on wood gave away his position.

A woman's voice shouted at the child, as the doctor left his car. "Denny, get yerself in this house right now."

The child responded with laughter, "I ain't taken no bath!" He plopped down in the dirt and wrapped himself around the beagle who chewed at the boy's arm.

Agnes Williamson appeared on the porch, her best drill sergeant voice in command, "Now, boy!" Merlene's mother wore a floral apron over a plaid housedress with a tea towel draped over her left shoulder. She caught sight of Jeremiah. "Hello, Dr. Henderson."

Jeremiah threw up a hand and headed for the errant lad. "Come on up here, Denny. Let's mind your grandma or she'll be mad enough to whoop us both." His extended hand grasped the smaller grubby one and they approached the porch. Two oblong stone boulders served as steps along the front. The doctor and his companion took the one nearest.

Denny left the grownups and dashed inside, the beagle pup barely making it through the screen door before it slammed.

Jeremiah offered his hand. "How're you holding up, Agnes?"

She shook, nodded and covered her mouth. After a moment she squeezed out a word, "Alright."

"I'm sorry for your loss. I don't know what else to say. Is there anything I can do to help?" A frown creased the doctor's brow.

"Nothin' I can think of right now." She glanced at the door as the noise of her grandchildren filtered outside. "Where's my manners? Come on in here and we'll have a cup of coffee. Tabby brought up a chocolate cake today, said it was yer favorite. Let me fix ye a slice of tha'." She'd pulled him inside the house, filled with comforting smells of cooking and the bountiful racket of six children's voices.

"Allow me, please." Jeremiah poured coffee while Agnes cut them each a piece of Tabby's finest cake. "Cream? Sugar?" He glanced up at Agnes' nod and poured fresh cream from a pitcher in the refrigerator. The cow had even been milked that morning.

He pulled out a chair for her and held it until she sat.

She lifted her coffee and sipped, working to contain her anxiety.

He sat and picked up his fork for a delectable taste of the fudge frosting. He laid it aside and patted Agnes' hand. "That's fine then. I sure have a good cook."

A smile broke on her face, even while tears spilled over her lined cheeks.

"I can't tell you it'll be alright, 'cause I can't guarantee that it will." He looked up to see one of the older boys come through to toss another log onto the fire in the stone fireplace. The boy glanced at him and nodded. "Jake, how're you holding up, son?"

"Alright, sir. Gotta take care of the others now."

Agnes opened her mouth to issue orders. "See to Denny and get him bathed. We need to make a run down the mountain."

"Yes ma'am." He speed-walked to the other end of the house where he followed his grandma's instructions. Denny kicked up a fuss and the beagle puppy bayed at the injustice of it all.

"Have arrangements been made?" Jeremiah wished there was a better way to ask.

She nodded. "We have family viewin' in an hour. They're bein' buried together. Rhonda Carson picked out a casket for a big man and they fit perfect side by side, with Merlene's arm though Earl's." She choked on a sob, but recovered quickly.

"Is there money for the funerals? Can I organize help? Just tell me whatever you need, I'll do it."

She shook her head. "They had burial policies. There's a little money left over fer headstones."

"What about for the kids?"

She shook her head again. "Not that much. I'm not sure how we'll make it. Prob'ly have to sell this place."

A spark flickered in a corner of the doctor's mind, but he pushed it aside. "We can get the state to help."

"We don't truck wi' charity. Ye ken that." She cut her eyes his way and her face reddened.

"I know. I just feel powerless and need the solace of helpin' you if I can." He sipped coffee and took another bite of cake. It felt like sawdust in his mouth.

"Earl built this place with his own hands." Agnes gazed around the kitchen, taking in the finely fitted logs. "He worked on it fer three years before he asked Merlene to marry him. They added on to it just as the second baby came." She looked into the flame of the fireplace. "Picked up ever' one of those stones and put 'em together like pieces of a puzzle. Dry fit, that's what he called it."

Jeremiah sat back and did all he could do effectively. He listened to her talk about the home filled with love, children and good memories. Christmas mornings with her grandchildren, birthday parties and Easter egg hunts took on an ethereal quality, as they do when a storyteller uses her craft to paint the pictures in her listener's mind. A century past, the clan's seanchaí, the one who passed on the lore, would keep the stories alive minus the arguments and fussing that usually occurred. The doctor smiled and closed his eyes to better see the canvas before him.

Chapter Three

Nurse Hill waited outside Marcia's room for the doctor to arrive. He left his hat and coat on the oak halltree by the front door and met her.

She came right to the point. "I think it's time for her to be moved."

"I've spoken with her family. They want her to come home. I have two weeks' vacation due. I'll prepare to return her to California." He met her eyes.

"You'll be stayin' with her there?" She worried the sleeve of her uniform, tugging on the cuff.

"As long as I can. I have to be here for my patients and the county. They pay the bills and I owe it to them."

"What do you owe her?" Nurse Hill's tone became sharp, her mouth drawn.

He glared. "I've given her almost six years of my life and been a complete disappointment, in most every way. But she's my wife. I took her from her family; I'll see she goes home to them. Hopefully she'll find some peace, before passing."

"Yes, sir." She studied the floor.

"If you want to go with her, you may and come home when—it's done."

Her head bobbed. "I will, sir."

"We'll leave here on Sunday, that'll be the ride she requested." He turned his back to the nurse and walked toward the kitchen, where Tabby O'Hern banged dishes and the aromas smelled like heaven.

Jeremiah sat in his study to consider the previous 15 hours. There was something he missed, some thought flitted through, but didn't stop to rest and he missed the implications. Something to do with property. He made a list of items to check at the county clerk's office in the courthouse. Agnes told him that Earl owned the 14 acres his grandfather gave him, upon graduating from high school. He began construction on the log house using timber and rock from the land and the tools his grandfather loaned him. There shouldn't be a mortgage on the place, but he wanted to know. He wrote the names of the other three sets of victims. As long as he was there, he might as well get the information on their property and what happened to it. There had to be a pattern somewhere and land was the most obvious. They all lived near each other on the mountain.

He doodled on the side of the page and his thoughts wandered. When the phone rang he sat forward and snagged the receiver. "Dr. Henderson speaking." Tabby was gone for the evening.

"Doc, this is Henry Phipps."

"Yes, Henry?"

"Ponderin' our conversation, I decided to look into that shop down in Athens. It's a big place; they turn out hundreds of cars a week. Got a crew of thirty techs that do nothin' but mufflers and exhaust systems."

"What are you thinkin'?" Jeremiah focused on Henry's voice.

"About takin' a run down there. I been dreamin' about those big chrome dual headers for my truck."

"Henry, please be careful."

"I will, Doc, just wanted you know I'm gonna run down there on Monday, when I close the garage."

"Keep me informed about what you find out and for Pete's sake, don't ask questions and let on like you're suspicious of their product or installation. You don't have a clue what you're walkin' into, pal."

"I'll be cool about it. Talk to you in a day or two."

"Do, please." Jeremiah lowered the phone and realized he'd be in California when Henry returned.

Chapter Four

The Boeing 727-95 landed sweetly on the runway at Los Angeles Airport with 96 passengers on board. Jeremiah shifted and checked on his wife, across the aisle with Nurse Hill.

Marcia moaned. "Thank God, that's over." She struggled to sit more erect with the nurse's help.

The doctor checked his watch. Time for more morphine. The nurse met his eyes, one brow raised. He shook his head. Marcia would have to endure the shift to a wheelchair and transfer to a vehicle before she could have an injection. He hated the decision, but more damage could occur to her fragile body if she failed to control some of her movements.

The doctor snugged his tie and prepared to leave the plane with his black bag at hand. He softly rested his fingertips on his wife's shoulder when he rose. "The chair will be here for you in a moment. I'll see to the luggage and meet you in the front of the airport. There should be a chauffeured car waiting."

"Alright. You won't be long?" She knew he governed the next dose of the heady drug that kept her sane.

"I should be there before you—barring delays." He felt pressured to move on by the queue formed behind him. He left the plane, meeting the stewards with the wheelchair on the tarmac. "Please, be very gentle with her. She's in a great deal of pain. Try to avoid bumps and unnecessary shifting."

"Yes, sir." The white suited black man nodded.

"Thank you." The doctor moved on swiftly to find their luggage and arrange for the car to be loaded.

Richard Matthews waited inside the luxuriously appointed Lincoln limousine. He attempted to read a contract, but kept lifting his eyes to the doorway. He pushed the paperwork back into his black leather briefcase and snapped it shut with a sigh. His driver stood ramrod straight beside the vehicle, eyes forward, watching for a sign of Jeremiah or Marcia.

When Marcia came in sight, Richard left the comfort of the car and met his invalid daughter. With his driver's assistance and the nurse's guidance the stewards moved the patient to the rearmost seat.

Jeremiah held the door open for the rack of luggage to be pushed toward the vehicle. He opened his black bag and handed over the vial and needle to the nurse. After swabbing the area with a cotton ball dipped in alcohol, she filled the syringe and injected Marcia Henderson.

Tense greetings were exchanged and everyone seated themselves for the journey. The limo proved the smoothest ride yet.

Richard muttered instructions to the driver through a telephone installed in a console against the seat back.

Marcia groaned with pain. Jeremiah turned to check her vital signs, for something to do that appeared connected to her illness.

Nurse Hill soothed her mistress' distress and tried to make her as comfortable as she could in a semi-reclining position.

"You should have brought her home sooner." Richard finally looked into his son-in-law's eyes.

"She didn't want to come. I had to convince her to make the trip. She's near the end, but she felt she'd live longer if she didn't leave *our* home. She may have been right. There's no telling what effect the change in altitude and barometric pressure has on the cancer. I do know the pain intensified." Jeremiah glanced out the pristine window at the sidewalks, cafes and restaurants passed on the street. He didn't miss the clutter or the inhabitants of cities.

The limo pulled into a half mile long concrete driveway to stop at the front of a Spanish Mission style mansion with jasmine and jacaranda climbing the trellises that framed the entrance. Moving Marcia inside became the focus, after the driver brought out her wheelchair and locked the brakes. He and Jeremiah worked together to get her safely moved. Her eyelids fluttered at one point and she smiled vaguely.

The driver pushed the wheelchair inside and headed to the rear of the vast entryway.

"We've installed an elevator." Richard flourished one hand toward a metal box.

He and Jeremiah followed by way of the wide sweeping grand staircase. "Thank you."

"She *is* my only daughter."

The doctor smiled at the slight. "You've never let me forget it, sir." They rounded the curve in the hallway and stepped into Marcia's bedroom.

Nurse Hill took over from the driver. They propped Marcia on her canopied full-size bed. The nurse was in the process of removing her shoes and clothes.

Richard turned back to the hallway. "Do join us in the study when she's settled."

"I will. Thank you." Jeremiah reached around his wife to pull her arm through a flannel pajama shirt. She was always cold.

Jeremiah found his father-in-law and third wife, Catherine enjoying cocktails in the study. Catherine wore a short silk shift over her tony tanned legs, much like a dress Marcia owned. She and Catherine were barely a year apart in age.

He accepted a highball glass from Richard. "Sit, Jeremiah. I want to clear the air and settle issues concerning my daughter right now. No need for the proverbial gray cloud to linger over us the duration of her short life, is there?"

The doctor sat on a tall leather covered side chair with brass nailhead trim. He leaned into the padded back and sipped the cocktail, checking for any traces of almond scent. Not that he suspected his father-in-law of such base designs. If he'd wanted to kill him, he would have done so five and half years earlier, before he married Marcia.

"I'm all ears. What needs to be settled?" He sipped the gin and tonic again, not his favorite cocktail, but any potion with numbing properties was welcome.

"Her inheritance, for one thing. Her mother left her well provided with a trust, as I'm sure you're aware."

"I remember that, yes."

"Well, I want the money channeled into cancer research as she—will have no further need of it—soon." Richard gulped down half of his g&t in one swallow. "Perhaps another poor woman won't have to go through all my daughter has endured. Perhaps there can be a cure found and her death won't be in vain." He turned his frown on his son-in-law.

Jeremiah watched through half opened eyes. "Mmm, she made arrangements for the funds to be spent on a new wing to the hospital in Delilah. You should speak to her about *her* wishes. Death is not futile unless the life lived was without hope. I'm sorry, Richard, I don't share your sentiments."

"Well, we'll see that altered, then." Richard knocked back the remainder of his cocktail. "I suppose the addition *she's* paying for puts a feather in your cap."

"No, it doesn't. If you recall we had a child. He was born far too early and the closest hospital to treat his weak heart and lungs was several hours away. Marcia's gift will assure that premature babies can be treated and their lives saved."

Edgy silence filled the room for a few moments. Jeremiah studied the fire, safely ensconced behind glass in the stucco and tiled fireplace. Catherine, a smile on her lips, sipped her cocktail.

"I have a meeting at my office." Richard spun on his heel and left the two of them sitting quietly.

After a lull, Catherine spoke, "I'll see that dinner is taken up to Marcia and her nurse. It may just be the two of us tonight, Jerry."

The doctor winced, at a nickname, no one but his wife ever used. His mother and friends called him Miah.

Jeremiah tried to shake off the tapping in his head. Suddenly alarmed, he bolted upright and threw the covers back. He pulled on his robe and opened the door, as he tied the belt.

Nurse Hill stood in the hallway. "I'm sorry, sir, but Mrs. Henderson is a bit on edge and insisted she speak to you at once." Jeremiah noticed curlers in her hair.

"Well, I'm behind you." He followed along barefoot.

Nurse Hill preceded him into her mistress's room. Her voice became low and calm. "There now, he's here, darlin'." She rounded the bed and sat at the edge, one leg hiked up, leaning toward her patient.

Jeremiah bent over his wife. Her breathing had become more labored in the hours since he checked her, before he retired for the night. "Marcia, I'm here. What can I do?"

She weakly patted her chest. "Can't breathe."

The rattle became more apparent. "I see. Well, we can try a menthol rub. I can set you up higher, have nurse prop more pillows around you…."

She shook her head, whispering, "Can you give me anything?"

"I don't feel it's safe." He switched on the bedside lamp.

She chuckled hoarsely, followed by a coughing fit. "Might it kill me?"

He slipped one arm under her pillow and lifted her, while Nurse Hill stuffed another beneath the first from her side of the bed.

"I don't know. The trip took a toll and I fear the worst just now. Can we try home remedies and see if they give you any comfort?" He met her dark eyes and realized the bags of fluid beneath them were heavier than usual. "Nurse Hill, would you go down to the kitchen and prepare Mrs. Henderson a toddy, please? Something warm with peppermint Schnapps might do the trick." He ventured a smile at his wife, as he regretted leaving his house slippers behind.

"Sir, there's a salve in the dressing table. I'll be back in a moment." She left them.

Jeremiah searched the drawer in the vanity and found Watkin's Menthol Rub. He unbuttoned Marcia's gown and slathered the liniment on her drawn flesh. He smiled at the memory of her firm, silky skin beneath his fingertips.

"What's funny?" She managed to squeeze out the words.

"Nothing." His eyes blurred with unshed tears. He had not allowed himself the smallest moments of grief until this one. "You'll probably have pneumonia by morning if we don't take you to the hospital. But – I leave the decision up to you."

Her voice could barely be heard. "No—want to die here, my bed—home. You—did your best." She watched him closely.

"I tried." He nodded and lightly touched her temple. His grandmother used Vick's Salve when he was sick, as a child, massaging it into his chest, on his temples and across his forehead. He did the same for his wife, moving slowly, cautiously.

The menthol burned her eyes. She closed them and attempted to breathe normally.

Nurse Hill came through the door with a steaming porcelain cup. "Here we are then, sir."

Jeremiah took the cup and tipped it to his lip, blew on the hot brew and tried it again. "I think it's cool enough to sip." He scooped a silver spoonful to his wife's mouth and she took it, still watching him.

"I can do this, sir." Nurse Hill stood at the ready.

He looked up. "Let me this time. You may return to bed. I'll sit with her here."

"Wake me if you need me?"

"I will do that."

She left them.

Once Marcia slept, Jeremiah situated himself in the chair beside the bed, covered with a shawl. He laid his hand beside hers on the fluffy mattress.

Morning cast sunshine through slits in the blinds onto the chair. Jeremiah winced, with a pounding headache and a stiff neck. He'd slept too soundly in an awkward position. He leaned toward his wife, checking her pulse as he couldn't see the rise and fall of her chest in the half-light covering her. Her heartrate was slow, but steady. A rattle sounded in her breathing when she stirred, moaning with pain at her own movement.

Nurse Hill appeared, smoothing the front of her white uniform. "If you'd like to retire, sir, I'll be right here with her."

"Why don't you go down, get breakfast and coffee. I can give her the morphine." He reached for the syringe and bottle.

She handed it over and left for the kitchen.

Marcia moved, a whimper in her voice, before she woke. "Jer?"

"I'm here, darlin'." He held the syringe to the light and filled it. "I'll give you your pain medicine now." His eyes met hers, barely slits. "Alright?"

She nodded slowly. "Alrigh…."

He inserted the needle and let the liquid flow into her veins. He'd fought his conscience through the night and decided to increase her medication in small increments to give her more relief. He glanced up into her eyes and considered the first time he kissed her. She kept her eyes focused on him. They studied each movement as though it would be the last time they saw each other, drinking in the intimate moment as husband and wife. He leaned to her lips and brushed a kiss over them.

He breathed close to her ear. "Can I get you *anythin'*?"

"No…." Her eyes closed and she slipped into momentary peace.

The door opened and Richard Matthews stepped inside.

Frowning, Jeremiah turned at the intrusion, not even a tap to alert them there was someone entering the room.

"I wanted to see her this morning. How is she?" He noticed his son-in-law was barefooted.

"Rough night." The doctor felt especially peevish. "If you want any time with her at all, you'll need to make it today." He rose and stepped away from the bed.

"Is she worse? Shall we call an ambulance?"

"She has pneumonia, but we discussed it in the wee hours this morning. She doesn't want to go to the hospital. If you'd prefer to send her, not have her die here, we can leave. I don't expect her to be aware of much today. But we can hold off the next injection due—" He checked his watch, "in six hours." He considered his father-in-law. "The nurse will return shortly. If you'd like to stay with your daughter, I'll go shower." He ran his hand over his scruffy face. "I don't want her alone for a moment."

Richard glanced up. "I will." He sat in the chair Jeremiah left.

The hot shower felt wonderful. Jeremiah reveled in the feel of the water on his skin. He shaved and dressed for the day in casual slacks and a pullover. He tied on boat shoes and left the room to check on Marcia again before heading downstairs.

Nurse Hill sat in the bedside chair, knitting in her hand. She spoke softly to her mistress. "Then when the rascal climbed that tree, he couldn't get back down. 'Got no down genes' my granny said and she may have been right. That cat was stuck until my Tommy came home from school and rescued him." She glanced up. "Sorry, sir."

"No need to be. How's she sleeping?"

"Seems to be as right as she can be. I fear she has pneumonia." She shifted a look his way.

He nodded. "Likely from the flight, but she won't go to the hospital. I told her father this morning. He may be back later to sit with her again before her pain medication. Give him all the privacy he requires. Things need to be said." He studied the toe of his shoe. "It may well be the last day we have her."

"I'll tend her, sir." She sat back and resumed her knitting.

A baby blanket is what it looks like, he thought, wondering if she had grandchildren.

After a cup of coffee and a piece of toast, Jeremiah went to the library to use the phone. He sat studying the instrument for a moment before he lifted the receiver and dialed his sister's number in Atlanta. She answered on the first ring.

"Hello, Ana. It's me." He sighed.

"Oh, darlin', is this the call I've dreaded for the past 18 months?" Her voice was soothing, always the nurturer of people and helpless animals. Of his three sisters Mary Ana Kraus was his favorite. The feeling was mutual.

"I'm afraid so." Tears flowed freely. He dug a handkerchief from his trousers' pocket. "We arrived in Los Angeles yesterday. Marcia appears to have pneumonia. She prefers to not go to the hospital and I see no need to treat it."

"Will it make—you know—the end easier?"

"And sooner. She's so very tired of it all. If I could help her along, I would but—"

"I know, sugar. I'll be there as soon as I can. Don't worry about Mama, Carol and Joy. Let me make the calls." He could hear the background noise of her moving around.

"Thank you. Phone here to be picked up or take a taxi."

She chuckled. "I'll take a taxi. The whole limo thing is kinda creepy. Down here we reserve those for funerals and weddings."

"I understand."

"Hopefully I'll see you by tomorrow morning." Silence quieted the phone line for a moment. "I want to get there in time to say goodbye. I'll not wait around for the others."

"Good, I need you here." When he replaced the receiver and turned, he found Marcia's father propped in the doorway.

"Gathering the troops already, are you?"

"Yes." Jeremiah nodded. "My oldest sister will join us soon. Richard, I really don't know if Marcia will last the day."

"Not if you *help her along*." The sneer he wore left no doubt to how long he'd listened to Jeremiah's conversation with Ana.

"I won't fight with you over my wife. Please, enjoy what time we have remaining." The doctor left the chair and headed to the front door. A walk would clear his head before returning to Marcia's bedside.

Thoroughly invigorated from the brisk stroll, Jeremiah climbed the stairs toward his wife. He'd picked a handful of wildflowers in a nearby meadow. He quietly opened her door to find Nurse Hill tidying the room.

She glanced up, with a smile and whispered, "I'll take those, sir." She reached for the crude bouquet and found a glass vase in a collection on the bookcase.

The doctor checked on his wife. Her breathing was ragged. She turned her head and coughed; congestion thick in her lungs. A touch on her cool forehead left him no doubts that her body had little energy to fight the infection.

Nurse Hill set the vase on the bedside table. "She's not stirred, but to cough occasionally."

"Take a break. I'll stay with her. There's a meadow the other side of the trees back that direction," He pointed beyond the lawn on the west side of the house. "And a walking trail through it, if you'd like. Take advantage of the sunshine. It's warm here." He smiled, the odd gesture tensing his facial muscles.

"I'll grab my walking shoes and take you up on it. Our winter's lasted too long this year. I could grow accustomed to warmth year-round, with my arthritis and achy joints."

"I agree." He parked himself in the bedside chair and picked up the book he'd borrowed from the downstairs library.

Jeremiah dragged himself out of a catnap. He replaced the book on the table and listened to his wife's breathing. She was still asleep. He plumped up the pillows to raise her position and the noise in her chest lessened.

The door opened to her father. "How is my daughter?" He walked to the side of her bed and felt her hand, lying loose on top of the quilt. "Is this death rattles?"

Jeremiah shook his head and placed a finger over his lips. "Shh. We talk, even when she's asleep, as though she hears our words. Sometimes she responds, when she wakes up."

"Oh, well, no worry of that at this point, eh?" He glowered at his daughter's unresponsive face.

Jeremiah sat. "We try and show as much respect for her as we ordinarily would."

"Well, I have a meeting to attend, important client, then I'll return and spend a little time with her."

"Alright. Nurse Hill or I will be by her side. She can't be alone." Jeremiah yawned and watched Richard leave, without further ado.

Nurse Hill returned from her walk, before the door closed. She whispered, "Sir, how is she?"

"Congested. I raised her head a bit more and it seems to help. Did you enjoy yourself?"

"I did, thank you. Is all the land on that side part of this estate?" She slipped out of her sweater and pulled on the white apron she wore over her uniform.

"Yes, down to the burn, um, stream on the opposite end." Something flickered in the doctor's memory. *Oh, to recall what I missed...when Agnes and I discussed—*

His wife's voice interrupted, "Jerry?" She battled her swollen eyes, her forehead wrinkled.

"Marcia, I'm here." He bent over her, kissing her forehead. "Do you need something?"

"Yeah." She struggled to take a deep breath, spawning a coughing fit.

Jeremiah scooped her off the pillows into a sitting position.

Nurse Hill grabbed a towel and kidney dish to catch whatever she could. She crawled over the bed on the opposite side and helped support her mistress. The bloody phlegm from Marcia's lungs almost filled the small stainless pan. The nurse left to empty it and bring back a damp bath cloth.

The doctor pushed another pillow behind his wife's shoulders. "Alright now, how about a drink of water?" He held the glass with a bent straw, glad that Nurse Hill packed all the necessary items of their daily lives. Marcia sipped through the straw, almost a quarter cup.

"Darlin', we're goin' to start an IV." Jeremiah glanced Nurse Hill's direction. She handed over the cloth and went for supplies.

"Must you?" She managed.

"You aren't getting enough fluid." He held up his hand when she began to protest. "You need more. You did well drinking yesterday and last night, but today you've barely had a cup. Your catheter bag is practically empty and that won't do."

Nurse Hill arrived with the paraphernalia and began by shooing the doctor from the area she needed to work.

He settled onto the bed beside his wife and kept her distracted while the nurse set the needle into the vein. Until the morphine, Marcia always had a fear of needles. There was no reason to distress her by allowing her to watch the IV set up. Nurse Hill had a light touch and was very accurate catching her patient's rolling veins, without more than one puncture. It was the main reason Jeremiah hired her.

The door opened and Richard stepped inside. "What's this?" He strode to the bedside.

Marcia rolled her eyes his way, just as Nurse Hill attached the bag of glucose. She gasped out a greeting, "Hello—Daddy. Welcome—to what life—becomes." She shuddered as another coughing fit struck her.

Jeremiah hauled her upright and Nurse Hill scampered for the kidney dish. Afterward, she mopped her mistress' face with the damp cloth, while the doctor made her comfortable on the pillows.

Richard stood at the end of her bed observing, until it passed. He inhaled and pursed his lips. "If you'd rather, I can leave."

Jeremiah spoke up, "Please stay. Now is an excellent time to visit. She's awake for a few minutes." He left the canopied bed and slipped his shoes back on. "I'll give you privacy; Nurse Hill will be at hand." He nodded to let her know she could step into the next room.

After changing his shirt for dinner and donning a jacket, he returned to his wife. Nurse Hill stood outside the door, leaning against the Venetian plaster wall. She inhaled and sighed, crossing her arms.

Jeremiah whispered, "What's happening in there?"

"Oh, sir." She straightened, glancing back at the door. "He's weepin' like a child. I hear her voice a bit. She's not called for me, so I decided to wait out here until he's done."

"Richard? Crying? Well, good. We all need to begin our grieving process while we have her. There are a lot of things that we need to say. I've made a list for myself." He patted his jacket pocket.

The door opened and Richard stepped through. "She asked for you." He glanced up at his son-in-law and wiped his eyes with a silk handkerchief.

Marcia was exhausted. "Jerry, please?" Her speech slurred. Her hand lifted slightly to motion him to the bed. "I need—meds."

"Alright." He watched Nurse Hill hurrying to her room.

Jeremiah lifted his wife by raising her pillow with one arm and stuffing another behind her limp form. "There, now." He smiled as tears ran down his cheeks and reached for Nurse Hill's outstretched hand.

His wife calmed as soon as the narcotic hit her blood stream. Her eyes closed and she relaxed only to be hit by a coughing spell. He scooped her forward until she caught her breath and laid her gently back on the pillows.

Ana tapped on the bedroom door. Nurse Hill ran her hand over her hair and opened to Jeremiah's sister. She stepped into the darkened room to find her brother on his feet, brushing his fingers through his dark, graying hair.

His whisper barely reached her, "Thank God, you made it!" He wrapped his arms around her and felt his clench on emotions running thin. A sob shook him and he held on tighter.

"It's alright, sunshine." Ana snuggled into his rough neck and spoke softly. "It'll always be alright." The long, drawn-out vowels of her Southern drawl were balm to his soul.

He nodded and pulled away to wipe his face. "How was your flight?"

"Pure hay-ell, but it served its purpose." She peeked past him at the rattling noise of Marcia's shallow breath. "Can I just see her for a minute?"

"Certainly, dear. She may not know you're here." He stuffed his hands in his trouser pockets.

Ana tiptoed to the bedside and propped her substantial frame beside her sister-in-law.

Amazingly Marcia's eyes opened and she mumbled. "You came."

"Wouldn't have missed a chance to see *you*, now, would I?" Ana stroked Marcia's hair away from her face.

"…to say goodbye." Marcia's eyes drooped closed and she moaned.

Jeremiah reached for her hand, as her body quivered, her eyes blinked and a final sigh puffed stale air out her mouth.

He stood there for a moment, stunned. In spite of the months to prepare for closure, he dropped to the chair's seat, his mouth agape.

Ana gently closed Marcia's eyes. She removed her brother's hand from his wife's and held it in her own. "We need to fetch Richard. He said he planned on coming up later but…."

"Yes, by all means." Nurse Hill hurried through the door.

"It's over, darlin'," Ana gazed into Jeremiah's confounded expression.

He nodded and caught a deep breath.

The door opened and Richard stepped inside. His voice sounded harsh in the dead stillness of the room, "Is it done?"

Ana's head tilted to one side. "Yes, Richard, it's over."

Chapter Five

Jeremiah sat at his study desk and sighed. The house was quiet as a tomb. He stopped briefly in town and picked up Lester from the lady who kept his dog when he made trips away from home. The yellow lab mix plopped in front of the cold hearth after they arrived. The doctor took a few moments and lit three fireplaces to shake the chill in the house.

He returned to his desk and looked over notes and scribblings on the blotter trying to pick up the train of thought he'd had two weeks earlier. *Something about property.* He organized his notes into one document. *Henry...Henry was going to Athens to have one of those fancy mufflers installed. I need to see him tomorrow.*

The day was bright and the sun shone down from a cloudless sky. Jeremiah slipped on sunglasses, before embarking on the journey, from his office to Henry's garage. He passed a few patients, tipping his hat to the vicar.

Henry was submerged beneath the hood of a Chevy Malibu. He lay on a quilted cover thrown over the engine, legs extended in midair. The radio blasted out a tune about a hard-loving woman and a good-timing man.

"Henry?" The doctor stopped short.

The mechanic slid off his perch and glanced around the hood. "Doc? Hey, sorry to hear about your wife." He wiped his hands on a blue rag.

"Thank you. I got home from California last night and was trying to work out where we were in the investigation of the carbon monoxide deaths. What'd you find in Athens?"

"Great set up they have there, as pristine as an operatin' room. I hung around as long as they let me, but got herded off to the customer lounge. I watched to see what I could from the window, but it wasn't much."

"Did you meet anyone you knew?"

"Nah, there's a strange feelin' to that garage: cold, sterile, nothin' outta place. But it's more than that. If I was superstitious, I'd say it was spooky." He looked up.

"If the deaths of six people were a direct result of the work they do, it's not superstition, it's good sense."

"Then there's that weird sensation of bein' watched. You ken, when you're alone and the curtain's open and you get creeped out passin'? The hair on the back o' your neck stands up and chills rush over your skin? Like that. I think I see somebody watchin' just out the corner of my eye, off to one side. When I turn to look it's just wind blowin' a bush or a person walkin' past. Strange." He fell silent for a moment. "Anyhow, I'm glad you're home. Seemed like I was on my own with nobody to watch my back. *And* I ride with my window down just in case."

The doctor nodded. "Understandable. Well, I don't really see any more paths opened to investigation, other than the property search. I'm headed over to the county clerk's office to see what happened to the land owned by the folks who died. There's somethin'—at the back of my mind I can't seem to reconcile."

Henry nodded. "Let's keep in touch. I have a bad feelin' about all this. Wish I could put my finger on the spot that bothers me the most, but it's vague."

"Well said, that. I sense the same. If it's a game, it's a conundrum, for sure."

The stroll to the courthouse was uneventful, until he opened the door and saw Junal Finley step out of the elevator, her eyes on an open file in her hands. He stopped, intending to hold the door for her, throw down his jacket or anything else he could do to get her to look up at him.

She closed the file and glanced around, her hazel gaze adjusted to include him and a smile crossed her face. "Well, Doctor, how're you doin' this fine mornin'?" She covered the few feet between them with grace, her heels clicking on the marble floor.

Jeremiah felt like the only man in the world just then, because *she*'d favored him with recognition.

"Fine, Miss Finley. And you?" He opened and held the door for her.

"Splendid now." She passed through, slipping on her sunglasses and turning back with a long gaze. "See ya later."

44

I wish. He thought. Darlin', I do want to see you later. A funny feeling caught him off guard. Not guilt exactly. Marcia's passed. I'll move on eventually…but not today.

Sitting in his office chair, he watched dust motes glisten in the stream of sunlight seeping through metal blinds. He glanced over the notes made at the clerk's office again. Other than Earl and Merlene's place, the other property had been purchased by a corporate entity, Firemaker Enterprises. He'd run up the mountain and see Agnes. Maybe an offer had been made on Carson's home and land. If not, it was another dead end.

He set out for the journey, keenly aware that he was probably not alone as he searched.

Agnes stood in the yard, the hem of her flour-sack apron gathered in her hand, while she scattered cracked corn to the chickens, round her feet.

Jeremiah parked the Buick in the driveway and watched her turn toward him shaking out her apron.

"Doctor Henderson, what a nice surprise." She met him halfway. "Let's go in the house. Supper's on." She stepped in ahead of him, while he held the wood framed screen door.

"How're you fairin', Agnes?" He pulled out a seat at the table.

She headed to the wood burning cookstove to stir a pot of soup.

"Fine, we're all fine." She turned to face him. "I'm sorry fer yer loss." Her forehead wrinkled with a thousand woes. Life was hard for women in the Appalachians.

"I'm doin' well. Thank you, though. I wondered, if y'all had any offers on the property yet." He leaned back and tried not to appear anxious.

"Herb and me decided we'd sell our place and keep this one, fer the young'uns sakes. He's movin' the herd down this week. If we cut half the timber here, we should have enough to get all the bills paid off and bank the rest."

"Has anyone been around to ask if you were selling?"

She studied the floor for a minute, before answering, "Now that you mention it, the sheriff came by about a week ago to see when the place would go up fer sale. I told him we weren't gonna do it that way. He left, seemed like he was in a bit of a huff, ye ken?" She pivoted back to the hot cast iron soup pot and scraped the bottom again.

"Really?" Jeremiah wondered why Sheriff Little was interested in buying property.

"Told 'im we'd be movin' here and sellin' our farm, but he just growled and climbed his fat ass—sorry…" She tossed the apology over her shoulder, "got in the car and left."

The doctor grinned and stood, the straight-backed chair legs scraping the floor. "How're the kids doin'?"

She sighed. "Jake wants to quit school and go to work at the mill. Says he feels like it's his part to help take care of the little ones."

"Agnes, don't let him do that." Jeremiah crammed his hands in his pockets. "Let me share somethin' with you that *cannot* go any further."

She met his eyes. "Like what?"

"You can tell Herbert, but no one else. Promise me." He was as stern as he could be.

She nodded.

"Daddy left a college fund for Jake. He had him in Scouts that last year he was alive, remember?"

She dried her hands on a dishtowel. "I recall that. It was Jake's first year; he was in fourth grade."

"Daddy felt like Jake was smart, but there was somethin' special about him. He said the boy was mechanically inclined in a unique way and he felt like, if he had the chance to go to college, the sky would be the only limit for him. If we don't guard that opportunity, Agnes, he could lose the money in the trust. Daddy set it up so that it would kick in, as soon as Jake graduates from high school. I'm executor of the trust, but there's no getting round the terms."

"Yer father, a doctor, did that fer *my* grandson?" Her face twisted into a frown.

Jeremiah realized his error. It might seem like charity. "He did it for several children through the years. He was never a rich man, except in love, but he had a fine talent for investing in the right—people to make more of what he had. Off the top of my head, I can name a lady who owns a diner, a dentist, a mechanic and an attorney here in town who benefited from Daddy's support."

She smiled. "Well now, that's truly somethin'." She faced the stove again, heartily stirring the soup. After a moment she looked back at Jeremiah. "We'll make it somehow, keep 'im in school, ye ken. We can do that." She sat the heavy pot off the stove onto a thick slab of granite.

"I can still get help with the children…." He spread his hands.

She smiled. "Ye're ornery, boy. I done said no once." She looked uncertain. "What kind o' help?"

"Not charity."

"Le's discuss it then." She pulled out a chair at the hand built wooden table and sat.

"I took the liberty of having Mary Ellen check into Earl and Merlene's Social Security accounts."

"Tha's fer retirement?"

"Also, to take care of children as long as they're minors. You can file and get the money that they paid in while they were both workin'. It'll not make anybody rich, but with six kids, it'll be a nice monthly stipend to help through the rough spots."

Agnes was nodding. "I can do tha'. Thank ye." Her worn hand covered Jeremiah's. "Thank ye very much, son."

Chapter Six

Mary Ellen stuck her head in the door of the doctor's office. "I put *your* mechanic in exam room three. He's a mess. I'll call for a nurse if you want me to."

Jeremiah left his desk and slipped into a freshly laundered white jacket. "Lemme look at him first." He strode through the door and ducked into room three. "What the hell?"

Henry tried to grin around his busted lip, two swollen black eyes and a seriously deep three-inch gash on his forehead. "Ran into a door."

Jeremiah washed his hands and approached the mechanic while he dried them. "Big door with big fists. You'll take stitches on the head wound."

Mary Ellen waited outside the room. "Need a nurse?"

"Nah, just get me a local anesthetic." Jeremiah laid out the instruments and pads required to patch Henry. "Tell me what happened."

Mary Ellen appeared with a vial and a spray, setting them both down on the stainless-steel rolling tray the doctor pulled alongside the exam table. She left as quietly as she came.

"I was out at the saloon last night." His words were garbled, as he held himself still for the needle that followed the freezing spray. "Trix waits tables out there."

"Uh-oh, woman troubles." The doctor smiled as he worked.

"Just minding my own business, Doc. Anyhow, she and that parasite, she lived with, been busted up for a week or so. She finally wised up and put him out." He winced at the burn of peroxide on a cut near his eye. "How 'bout waitin' 'til all tha's numb?"

"You're a wimp." Jeremiah grinned.

"Tha's true and I don't care who knows."

"So, did whozit show up? What's his name?"

"Ben. Yeah, one of his buddies I played pool with, called him after I beat him the third time. It was *his* idea to put money on the game, by the way."

"Okay. I thought Ben and Trixie were married."

"Nah, just shackin' up. She's way too good for the likes of *any* of those Brennons."

Jeremiah poked around the laceration near Henry's hairline. "Feel tha'?"

"No sir. So, she brought me a beer and grinned. I winked at her and Ben burst through the door. He made for me like a mad bull."

"You're a decent fighter, what does he look like this morning?"

"I didn't lay a hand on 'im." Henry allowed the doctor to tilt his head to one side.

"Why not?" Jeremiah pulled the sutures across the gash.

"Psychology, Doc. Think about it. If I hurt him, who's she going to nurse? Him of course. However, if it's me takes the beatin', I get the girl." Henry tried to smile, but it hurt too much.

Doctor Henderson chuckled as he took another stitch. "You're brilliant sometimes, but you didn't fight back *at all?*"

"No sir. Next time, I'll beat 'im to a pulp, but this time I had to show her how much I cared about her. There's no way to do that except takin' the thrashin' she was in for, if the jackass caught her in the parkin' lot after work. Anyhow, Quinn was there and hauled Ben off to jail."

"Quinn?" Jeremiah stopped midair and an idea fermented. "MacAdams?"

"Yes sir, the deputy. Oh, and Sheriff Little was there, too. A spooky fellow was with him. Somebody said it was his brother-in-law. Seen 'im somewhere before."

"Be still a minute." He tied off the suture and took a look at his handiwork. "Not as fine an embroidery job as your mamma might do, but it looks pretty good. You'll have a nasty scar."

"Worth it."

"So, where have you seen Little's brother-in-law before?" Jeremiah cleaned around Henry's eyes. "Sorry, no anesthesia for this."

"I can handle it. I saw 'im at that muffler shop in Athens." He shivered when the wound, at his left eyebrow, opened afresh from the cleaning. "Runs the whole shebang I think."

"Interesting. Agnes Williamson told me Sheriff Little came up to the Carson place askin' about buyin' it."

"What would he want with all that land? I thought Earl had almost twenty acres."

"Fourteen according to his mother-in-law. A gift from his grandpa. She and Herbert are taking over the place, to keep the kids at home."

"Good, tha's good, Doc." Henry's eyes closed, unbidden tears inching down his face. "Damn, that hurts worse than the beatin', I think."

"It'll take a few days for the swelling to go down. Put some ice cubes and water in a bowl and dip a washcloth in. Lay it over your eyes until it stops bein' cold and dip it again. Keep doin' that and the swelling will decrease faster. Try to keep it up, about fifteen minutes every hour, if possible. I can give you somethin' for pain."

"No sir, I need to be sharp, keep my wits about me, you know."

"I agree, however…you might at least take a couple of days off." Jeremiah dried his hands.

"Today, maybe tomorrow. I'm waitin' for a part to come in anyhow."

The doctor stepped to the door. "Mary Ellen, we need to show Henry how to make and use a cold compress, please."

"I'll get the bowl and ice for you." She set about her task.

"Do you have any back up help?" The doctor left the door cracked.

"There's Leo. He's still in high school, but fair at turnin' a wrench."

"Call him in. You're risking your vision, if you develop a blood clot in one of your eyes. I don't want you to be alone, Henry."

"Can take care of myself, Doc."

Jeremiah's voice dropped. "There's more than Ben and his friends goin' on here. Let me find out what connection there is to Sheriff Little, in all this. Quinn may be a good starting point. I'll give him a call today."

Henry glanced up, his head tilted back so he could view the doctor from the slits he looked through. "Hadn't thought o' that. Good idea. I'll close the shop until Leo gets out of school. Won't affect business a whole lot. Most folks call first."

"Let me take you home." Jeremiah slipped off his slightly soiled white jacket and tossed it into a hamper.

"No sir. Trixie's here, in the waitin' room."

Mary Ellen entered with a porcelain clad aluminum basin half filled with ice cubes. "Alright, Henry, let me show how to do this and we'll let you go." She ran a pint of water into the basin, wet a clean white hand towel, dipped it, wrung the water out and laid it on his head. "Now, hold that until it's not cold anymore and then go to the next wound. When your whole face is done, start again. Reapply the cold compress every other hour for the next two days. Do you understand, or do I need to write it down?"

"I ken your meanin' Miss Mary Ellen." Henry slid off the exam table, adjusted his trousers and headed to the waiting room.

"And don't go out drinkin' tonight." Jeremiah added, as he finished making notes in Henry's chart and placed it on Mary Ellen desk.

"Yes sir!" Henry called back, throwing up one hand, in retreat.

***

"Quinn?" Jeremiah recognized the deputy's voice when he answered the phone. "Jeremiah Henderson here."

"Hey, Doc! What can I do for you?" The big man sounded cheerful.

"I need to see you…privately. Is there any way you can come by my office, today or tomorrow?"

"I can swing by in an hour, if it suits you."

"Thank you, sir." The doctor replaced the receiver and considered organizing his thoughts. He picked up a pen and began to make notes for the meeting.

Former sheriff Quinn MacAdams was 6'9 and easily weighed 260 pounds, his light auburn hair was nappy, his skin the color of fresh caramel. His mother was white and his daddy black, not an odd thing in a small community in the Appalachian Mountains. In 1940 Sergeant Ronnie Hampton was stationed in England and met a Scottish army nurse, losing his heart to the busty redhead. He married her and took her surname as his own. It didn't make his skin lighter, but it stopped most awkward questions, before they were asked. His only son, Quinn followed in his parent's footsteps through army life. He left, on a medical discharge when his hip was shattered by the fragment of an exploding shell. The army called it friendly fire, but the men who were left in the unit, all wounded and discharged, lived with the results.

"You stitch Henry back together?" The deputy settled into the only substantial seat in the office.

Jeremiah smiled and leaned back in his swivel chair. "I did. Took a hell of a beating."

"Couldn't figure why he let Brennon whoop 'im like that. I've watched Henry in the boxing ring; he's lightning fast with those fists. Pretty sure he ain't slowed down, to the point a big fellow like Brennon could get the best of 'im."

"I said the same thing, but his idea was that he'd get the girl to nurse him back to health. Must be so, she brought him in here."

"Had to let Ben out this mornin' so he could go to work." Quinn stretched his long legs.

"I thought he was a bum," Jeremiah frowned.

"His brother got 'im a job down in Athens at a muffler shop. Pays well, so he thought he could land Trixie for *another* chance. Boy's sorrier than thrice-used grease."

"Muffler shop?" Jeremiah leaned forward and tried to not look anxious.

"Yeah, there's a big outfit that manufactures and installs those fancy tailpipes you hear disturbin' the peace. Sheriff's brother-in-law owns it, does rather well, if you get my drift." Quinn's brows rose, his tone dry.

"Ah, yes. Actually, that brings me to the reason I wanted to talk to you. How's the atmosphere in the department, since Little stole the sheriff's race from you?"

Quinn sighed. "Still say he cheated, though I can't prove it. At best it's tense when we're both in the office at the same time. I can take orders from anyone wearin' a uniform. Just bidin' my time. He'll screw up, before long, and I aim to take 'im down when he does."

"I'm quietly looking into the carbon monoxide deaths of eight people in less than six months. After the Carsons died, I pulled files on the previous three incidents. There's a lot they have in common, but we weren't suspicious enough, with the first two, so the paperwork is incomplete at best." Jeremiah leaned across the desk.

The deputy's voice quietened. "The sheriff investigated those, if I recall correctly."

"Yes, and he came by, after I requested the files, to see what I wanted with them. To discover his brother-in-law in the business he's in, makes me wonder about the first two cases and if there were new mufflers involved."

Quinn studied the floor for a moment. "Could be. I don't know what to tell you, but that those cars are long sold for scrap.

Nobody wants to buy a car that killed people." Quinn paused and glanced toward the window. "Even worse, the next case may be drivin' around the square as we speak."

"True." Jeremiah propped his chin in his hand and gazed out the open blinds, admiring Ratchet Mountain towering like a dark blue-green sentinel, over their small community. "Keep your head down, Quinn. Let's get together occasionally, as quietly as possible. Would it be conspicuous for you to come by the house?"

"Probably not as much as droppin' in here at the office. Don't do much business at the hospital."

"Didn't consider that. From now on we'll meet at my house. No need to draw attention to your place. I'm isolated and the trees, by the road, block the view. Too, be mindful of your wife and kids. I'm not sure where all this is leading. If it gets too hot, we don't need our loved ones involved."

Quinn smiled slyly. "You were a medic in Nam weren't you?"

"Yes, and you were an MP?"

"Believe we get too comfortable, in our secure little village, and forget bad people are out there lookin' for fools, the unwary and idiots to take advantage of. We're the perfect target for a smooth operator. I see boogie men behind most bushes. Hate to sound cynical, but I don't trust more than a half dozen folks around here, and I live wi' four of 'em." He levered his large frame from the armchair and stepped to the window to peer down into traffic coming and going from the hospital's entrance. He spotted a man leaning against a new vehicle smoking a cigarette. "Well, my goodness, speak of a devil." Quinn grinned.

Brow furrowed, Jeremiah joined him. "Who is he?"

"New deputy. Just so happens, he moved up here from Athens." Quinn slipped his hat on and turned to the door. "I'll take the back stairs." He closed the office door gently.

Jeremiah watched as minutes ticked past. He caught sight of Quinn approaching his squad car, from the farthest corner of the parking lot. He climbed in, backed out and left the watcher intent on the front entry.

Jeremiah returned to his desk. *This is becoming scary.*

Mary Ellen's voice crackled over his intercom. "You have a patient in room four, are you ready?"

"Be right there." He snagged a white coat from the rack and slipped it on.

Chapter Seven

One Month Later

"There was special mail fer ye today." At home, Tabby O'Hern handed the doctor his daily correspondence.

"Thank you, ma'am." He switched on the green-shaded banker's desk light and sat on the wooden swivel chair that was his father's and his grandfather's before him. The first envelope looked like an invitation. He sat it to one side and opened more pressing bills and letters, sorting as he went.

"Yer supper's in the stove. I'm headin' home." Tabby strode from the room, once she heard his customary grunt.

When he became aware of what she said, he hollered after her, "Thanks, Tab, have a good evenin'."

"Aye, sir," Came her shout from the back door.

Lester, his dog, lay down beside his chair, rolling his big brown eyes up at his master's movement.

"We'll go for a walk in the field directly, ol' boy. See if you can scare up a rabbit or two." Jeremiah tore the envelope of the invitation. "Hah! Bobby Finley's turnin' forty. How 'bout that?" He chuckled and realized that meant he was a year closer himself. "Oh my, Junal's goin' all out, with a dance and everythin'.

Hmm." He glanced down at his faithful companion. "Reckon they'd let us both in?"

Lester yawned and wagged his tail.

"Guess you can't be my date, heh." He scratched the heavy stubble on his neck and considered the lady giving the party. "I wonder if she'd have a dance with me." He checked his desk calendar and made a note of the date and time, three weeks hence. "Mama'll be here tomorrow, Lester, so you'll have company all day for the next two weeks. She calls it spring cleaning, but I know her. She's up to somethin'."

At midday Jeremiah pulled into his driveway to find a red Ford Mustang convertible parked beside his mother's car. "Now, who could this be, I wonder?"

He opened the gate to meet Lester, wagging all over and a black and white cocker spaniel yapping, standing her ground on the front steps.

"I live here, puffball." The doctor walked around the dog and into the house, allowing the screen door to slam shut behind him, one of the many sounds he'd missed when Marcia was sick.

"Hullo!" Margie Henderson stuck her head around the corner from the kitchen. She grinned as her son walked through the dining room. "If you're here for lunch, it's no' made yet and Tabby's in Atlanta for a few days, for the birth of her sixth grandchild."

"I smell paint." He proceeded and stepped inside the freshly painted daffodil yellow kitchen, stopping dead in his tracks.

"Thought we'd brighten it up a bit." His mother wiped her wet hands on a tea towel and followed her son's gaze upward. "Junal took the day off to help me."

June Allison Finley stood barefooted on the edge of the counter to reach a corner over a transom window. "Hello, Miah." She glanced back and smiled.

His heart melted and his body flushed. "Hello, Junal. This is beautiful." She turned back to her work so he could admire her perfect bottom in snug, shabby, paint-stained jeans.

His mother responded. "Mmm, I like the color on the walls, too." She smiled knowingly and stepped between him and the object of his lust. "I'll make sandwiches."

He nodded and took a few steps closer to Junal. "You're right on the edge of the counter. Watch yourself."

"Just…done. There we are." She held an artist's brush aloft and scanned the area around the transom. "Could you push the stepladder this way a bit, please?" She smiled beguilingly, while he did her bidding.

He instinctively reached out to steady her descent. Her skin felt warm through her thin tee-shirt, her face flushed from the encounter—or the heat at the top of the room.

Once her beautifully manicured bare feet touched the floor, she gazed up into his eyes. "Thank you, sir." She spun to the sink and began washing up. "We'll be finished before dinner." She turned back and found a towel to dry her hands, while she watched him stuff his into his pockets and look away.

"That'll be fine then. Is that your spaniel guardin' the steps?" He couldn't meet her striking hazel eyes with the thoughts crowding his mind.

"Tha's my Daisy, yes. She and Lester like each other, so I brought her up with me. I hate to leave her cooped up inside, all day, when she can be out enjoyin' the sunshine." She hung the towel on a rack beneath the sink. "I hope you don't mind."

"No, not at all. She's a good watchdog." He strolled the perimeter of the kitchen inspecting the new wall color.

"She is. What do you want to drink, Doctor?" Junal opened the fridge and produced a glass pitcher of tea and one of lemonade. She looked right at home in his kitchen.

"Junal squeezed lemonade for us, Miah. Have a glass, it's delish." His mother cut sandwiches into triangles. "I brought pumpernickel and rye breads this time." Quiet settled for a moment. "It's such a lovely day. Let's sit on the back porch. Grab a tablecloth and napkins, son."

Jeremiah hurried to his mother's request and had the cloth covering a wooden table, as old as the house, by the time the ladies joined him. He held his mother's chair and seated Junal, when she was ready.

"Two lovely ladies and I don't have to eat lunch at Sally's today. I like this. Sure you don't want to move back, Mama?" He tucked his tie into his shirt front.

"I'd rather you get married and give me grandchildren."
Margie took a big bite of her sandwich and watched her son and
her friend blush.

They couldn't even look at each other.

Jeremiah knew his mother would think it was an excellent
indication she was on the right track.

***

"Going to bed," Margie Henderson called to her son as she trod
the heart pine floor down the hallway. "Don't forget that I'll be at
Ana's for a few days. Rose is riding down with me as far as
Bobby's. Tabby'll be back some time tomorrow."

"Yes, ma'am. See you in the mornin'." He sat at his desk and
checked the calendar. "Says here I have to see the attorney
tomorrow. Perhaps I'll ask Junal if she'd save a dance for me at
Bobby's party." He checked on Lester. "Okay, enough o' this,
let's go for a walk, boy." He pushed the chair back and stood.

Lester stirred, stretched and beat his master to the back door.

Damn, I haven't been this nervous since high school. His hand
drifted to his tie and he straightened it for the tenth time, since
leaving his office. He cleared his throat and opened the heavy oak
and glass door emblazoned *Lee, Compton and McDade, Attorneys
at Law* in gold lettering.

The receptionist was a pretty girl, in her twenties. Her name plate on the desk in front of her read Melissa McDade. She brightened with a smile. "Doctor Henderson, I haven't seen you since I had strep throat, in eleventh grade."

He grinned and nodded. "If I remember correctly, it wasn't strep, but mononucleosis and it was about a week before that I diagnosed Randy—"

Her left hand flew up and she giggled. "Enough already, that was ages ago. Besides we're engaged now." She displayed her diamond ring, making it official. "Daddy's waitin' for you." She stood and he followed her down the hallway.

He knew when he passed Junal's office. He smelled her perfume and thought he must be mad, to think a girl that lovely would be interested in a man a year from turning forty years old, any way other than a friend.

Carl McDade was on his feet, heading for the door with his hand extended. "Miah! How are you, old man?"

The comment didn't help Miah's drooping ego.

Melissa disappeared.

Carl's grin reminded the doctor of a used car salesman. They shook hands and exchanged greetings.

"I'm sorry, I'm gonna have to scoot. My youngest boy is bein' scouted by Bear Bryant, himself, today and I wanna be on hand. Listen though, Junal has the paperwork and she can answer any questions you have about the contractors and all that. She's handlin' the whole affair. Come on, I'll show you to her office."

Jeremiah smiled and followed obediently. God must be pleased with me today. This is easy.

Carl stopped, at the open door, and politely tapped on the glass. "Junal, Jeremiah's here and ready to go over those papers with you." Carl ushered him into the space, barely half as large as his own office. The big man patted the door frame. "I'll see y'all later."

The doctor dared lift his eyes to meet the paralegal's. "Junal, how are you?" He reached across her deskful of neatly stacked papers to offer his hand.

She retained her seat and smiled, her eyes sparkling. "Did you get your invitation to Bobby's birthday party?" She softly grasped and held his hand a moment, before releasing him.

He glanced down at the chair he lowered himself into. "I certainly did. Thank you."

"Are you coming?" She persisted; one elegant eyebrow arched.

He nodded. "Planning on it—if the babies due that week can take a break, so can I." He found himself feeling awkward, as she always conjured a smile from him, regardless of his mood.

She patted the stack of papers, her voice silky, "This was a noble thing your wife did, leavin' that money to the hospital to build a wing just for babies."

He glanced at the floor a moment. "She was capable of noble things. They were rare and I believe the donation originated more from guilt, than a higher moral cause. Our son died...."

"I know, born prematurely, wasn't he?" She propped her chin in her hand and studied him.

"He was…and not Marcia's fault. Not that way. She, uh, didn't wanna be pregnant."

They sat in silence a moment, Jeremiah struggling to understand why he told her that secret. *Stupid!*

She turned her wrist to check her watch. "Are you on a lunch break? Because I have the paperwork packed up, if you wanna buy me lunch." She wore a burgundy sheath and lipstick that was only a shade lighter. She stood and left the back of the desk, tucking a leather portfolio under her arm.

Jeremiah met her, trying his best to form an answer. "I...I... I would love to buy your lunch." *Today, tomorrow, for the rest of my life.*

A coquettish look swept over her face and she wet her lower lip. "Good, I thought you might say yes." She rested her hand in the loop of his arm and they left the building.

"Doc, you wanna warm up on that coffee?" Sally held the coffeepot over the table expecting an affirmative answer.

"Yes, thank you, and a piece of your cherry pie, too, Sally. Junal, dessert?" He gladly watched her consider the extra calories.

"May I have a bite of yours?"

"Certainly." He glanced up to catch the grin Sally pulled as she left. "Now, where were we?"

"They break ground the twelfth of November. I know that's not a great time of year to begin a project of this magnitude, but that's the earliest date we can have the entire crew from Murdoch's."

"You were engaged to Jim Murdoch, weren't you?" Jeremiah felt his face flame.

She observed his discomfort and fiddled with her napkin. Sally appeared with an ample slice of cherry pie and a scoop of vanilla ice cream on the side—with two spoons. The heavy China dish was parked in the center of the table.

"Thank you! Wow, this looks delightful." Miah fought the urge to lift the spoon to Junal's mouth. "Perhaps I shouldn't have broached the subject of your former relationship with Murdoch but—"

"No, it's okay." She smiled shyly. "We were engaged for a year and three months. I broke it off, but it was amicable. He knew he wasn't really *the one*, at least that's what he said."

"Oh." His heart sank. *There's someone special.* "I didn't mean to pry."

"Look, if we're going to work together, we need to come to an understanding." She leaned forward for a spoonful of the pie and chewed slowly. She studied the menu above the diner's counter and then back at him. "I broke it off with him when I heard there was a chance you were comin' back to take over your daddy's practice. Then, the rumor of someone else takin' that slot and you marrying a California heiress circulated." Her cheeks reddened. "I

67

dated again after that." She took another bite of pie and let what she said sink in.

"And then?" He prompted her, his mouth open and spoon poised in midair.

"Then I heard your son died and Marcia had terminal cancer. I won't lie and tell you I was sorry for the news." She sighed, leaned back in the booth and crossed her arms with a sigh. "Jeremiah Henderson, I've waited for you my whole life." Her smile was gone and her eyes misted.

His voice was low and hoarse. "*You* waited for *me*?" One eye was almost closed when he was confounded. "Hell, girl, I was just hopin' you'd dance with me at your brother's birthday party! I've been working up the courage to ask you for two days."

Junal reached across the table and removed the poised spoon from his hand to replace it on the bowl. "Honestly, for an intelligent man you're as dense as a concrete block." She dabbed her eyes with a mysteriously produced fine linen hankie, so as not to muss her makeup.

"Thank you." He sat there, dumbly watching her, then remembered they were opening their souls to each other. "I, um, have had a crush on you since you were thirteen. Was concerned I was a pedophile." He glanced around the diner to be sure they weren't being overheard. "I mean, I was so much older and…look, can we discuss this over dinner tonight?" He checked his watch.

"Oh, how selfish of me! I'm sorry. I forgot you need to get back to the hospital." She packed her portfolio.

He caught her hand, as she reached for another sheaf of papers. "At my house, say six? I'll call Tabby and have her prepare something wonderful and we can take a walk and…. talk 'til midnight."

She raised her gaze to his. "Absolutely. Shall I wear jeans?" Her head tilted in a certain way, that she could not know made his heart beat faster.

"Or you can change at the house. There's lots of privacy. Mama ran down to Atlanta to see Ana. I don't mean to sound like—" He raised his hand from hers. "Just old friends having dinner together."

"We won't be ships passing in the night?" Her look held hope

"Absolutely not—not *passing* at all." He checked the bill, Sally discreetly deposited on the table, removed a twenty from his wallet and laid it on top. "Come, I'll walk you back to work." He stood and reached for the portfolio, as she slid her tony bottom over the bench.

He enjoyed every moment of their walk and could hardly contain himself, as the afternoon dragged past and patients flowed through his office.

Chapter Eight

Jeremiah placed a stack of select records on the turntable. He chose some of the LP's from his parents' collection of dinner music, Frank Sinatra, Dean Martin, Martin Denny and Roger Williams. He lit candles that Tabby stuffed into his mother's freshly cleaned crystal candleholders and tried to recall the last time he'd eaten a meal at home, by candlelight. He couldn't recollect anything, as a married adult. Marcia preferred restaurants to home cooked fare—another disappointment, as there weren't any really fine restaurants in the area.

The crunch of gravel announced Junal's car pulling up the driveway. He hurried to open the door and glanced back to be sure everything was perfect, unrolling his shirt sleeves.

He watched her walk up the front path with Daisy in tow, and stepped out. "Welcome." He almost added *home*. He reached for her traincase and opened the screen for her to pass through.

"Thank you. I stopped off long enough to fetch Daisy and grab jeans and shoes. I hope you don't mind." She stepped into the light. "I left the office as soon as I could get away."

He met her smile and wanted to kiss her. "No problem. I'll put your bag in Mama's room." He started down the hallway.

"There's wine in the kitchen, pour us a glass?" He dropped her case on the bed and returned.

She handed the crystal stemmed vessel to him. "The kitchen looks great. I hope you like it. I chose the color." She sipped the white wine.

"Then I love it." He fought the heady sensation of being alone with her.

"What did Tabby leave us? I'm starved."

"Something wonderful. There's a salad in the fridge and I just set the casserole out for five minutes and I'm warming plates. She left written instructions."

Junal chuckled. "She *is* a treasure."

"Don't know what I'd do without her. She's been here all my life. After Ana was born Mama quit work and stayed home, but then Carol was born soon after Ana turned one and then Joy made her debut, and Mama was overwhelmed. So, Tabby came on board to help with babies and cook our meals." He pulled plates from the oven and set them on a Georgia marble topped island. He met Junal's eyes and sighed. *It's gonna be a long evening—I hope.*

They laughed over the salad, nibbled the cheesy Italian casserole and killed two bottles of wine. The sun had set and dusk settled with a fine haze of moisture suspended in the air.

"Tell me about Bobby." The doctor sat back in his chair.

"He's still…not over the war. He married an Army nurse. They won't be procreating as he's too afraid of his behavior, when he becomes stressed. He worked for a Ford dealership for a few years, but had to leave because…well, he couldn't handle the pressure."

"I'm so sorry, Junal. I'd hoped he'd be through the worst of it, by now."

"No." She straightened her silverware and napkin. "He's so sad sometimes; it just breaks my heart for him."

"Yeah, I can understand that. Is he able to work?"

"Sure, he has a part time job right now at a muffler shop. He works the slow-paced days. The owner was in Viet Nam too, and understands Bobby's…illness."

"Good. If there's anything I can do—"

"No, but thank you very much for saving his life. I've never had the chance to tell you. I haven't brought it up, because he hates talkin' about the war."

"I don't mind. You are welcome, but I didn't save his life. He saved mine. If he hadn't been hit, I'd've been in the midst of the shelling. As it was, I made a run for him, when he fell and was out of the way when a rocket blew my position to bits. We missed our walk." Jeremiah cleared the plates.

Junal followed with silverware and wineglasses. "Maybe tomorrow?"

He turned, after depositing plates in the sink, took silverware from her hand and brushed his lip over hers quickly. "I can make coffee. There's no way you're driving down the mountain after all that wine."

"I'm barely tipsy, Doctor." She touched his shoulder and looked up into his eyes. After a moment of studious perusal, she stretched to meet his lips and kissed him properly, long, gently. She stood down, but kept hold of his shoulders. "I've wanted to do that for twenty years."

His hands quivered as he held her waist. "Me too, Junal. I think I fell in love with you the first time we met. Do you remember?"

"I was playin' on a tire swing in the backyard and you came to see Bobby. The two of you tossed a football back and forth and talked about cars and girls. I burned with jealousy, Miah." She smoothed the fabric of his shirt under her hand. "When I heard you'd married it nearly killed me." Her voice broke. She met his eyes.

"If I'd known, I would've come home to you. You're really good at keeping secrets, heh?"

"Sometimes a girl has to be, in order to survive. I wasn't old enough to declare my undying passion for you. Daddy would've had a cat, if I'd talked to you for more than a minute. Even when you and Bobby came home from the Army, I was still too young to love you. But, love you I have. I've tried to—stamp out the memory of every look, every gesture we've traded through the years, but it's never worked. I've tried to love other men. That's been a dismal failure." She plucked at the buttons on his shirt and smiled shyly.

Jeremiah blushed. "You've yanked my chain your whole life. From the moment we met, I was tagged. In medical school, a friend introduced me to Marcia. I heard you were engaged and thought you lost to me. She pursued, envisioning a rich doctor's existence, when all I wanted was to come home and take care of my people, in the mountains. We were polar opposites and that caught up with us, before the first year was through." He sighed. "Does it need more explanation or can we put that bit behind us and start fresh?"

She laid her forehead on his chest. "Let it go and start fresh." She stepped back and extended her hand. "June Allison Finley, pleased to make your acquaintance, sir."

He caught her hand and pulled her closer. "Very pleased to make yours." He hugged her. "Let's have coffee."

They sat on the swing, on the front porch and watched mist roll in, the clouds lowering to shroud the mountaintop with a wet security blanket, creating a deserted island for the two of them. They held hands, sitting close enough their thighs pressed. The coffee warmed the chill that came with nightfall.

"Will you stay tonight? If you feel you must go home, let me drive you down the mountain. I can fetch you to your car—I can bring you back up in the morning."

"I can stay. Mom's down in Athens, at Bobby's for the weekend, so it was just Daisy and me anyway."

"Mama left clothes. I think she's moving back in, at least part time. You can find a gown and have her room, if you want."

"Do you sleep in the—same bed—well, that—"

"No, I moved into my old room four years ago because of emergency phone calls at night. Mama kept the master and Marcia—chose Joy's room."

"I see." She sat forward and stretched. "I'm a tad chilly. Would you build a fire for us?" She left the swing and they returned inside.

The dogs stretched out, on the hand braided wool rug in the living room. Jeremiah knelt in front of the fireplace and laid a fire. He struck a match and lit cured kindling beneath oak logs. When he turned, he found Junal on the sofa watching him. He loved the look in her eyes, soft, sexy and his…hopefully.

He joined her, turning to face her. "Tell me why you left law school."

She swung her foot over her crossed legs and laid her head back on the sofa pillow. "Daddy got sick. Mom needed help with the store. Bobby took off and didn't let anyone know where he was. He was away for more than two years. Mom couldn't do everything, so I quit. A year later we sold the store, and I thought about going back to school, but Daddy was still sick. I went to work at the law firm, with more formal education than most paralegals, but it's served me well."

Her hand slowly stroked his thigh like it was the first time she'd enjoyed the texture of denim.

"Do you still wanna go back to law school?" He caught a strand of her silky short hair between his fingers.

"I consider it occasionally. But I hope I won't."

"Why's that?" He brushed his fingers through her hair and watched her eyes.

She smiled and leaned into his kiss. "Tha's why."

He wrapped his arm around her and lifted her to his lap. He knew she could feel him pressing into her hip, but he didn't care.

"Miah?" Her voice was soft in his ear.

"Wha'?" He was lost in the scent and feel of her warmth.

"Make love to me?" She nestled her face against his neck.

He groaned. "I can do that." He rose, with her in his arms, and carried her down the hall.

He stood her on her feet, sat on the side of the bed and pulled her between his legs to unbutton her blouse. When he reached to unhook her bra, his face rested between her ample breasts. "Mmm." His hands moved down to her jeans and he smoothed them past her hips. He left them around her ankles to tackle a pair of lacy bikini panties. He slowed, to enjoy the sensation of her supple buttocks.

She gasped and caught her breath, her hands in his hair.

He glanced up and rose to kiss her, exploring her mouth with his tongue, while he loosed his jeans and pushed them down, with Junal's help.

When she encountered his erection pressing into her abdomen she wrapped one hand around him.

He nearly lost control and had to reinforce his restraint. He turned and led her onto the bed and lay beside her. Propped on his elbow he caressed her bare body. He was lost in a dream he'd had a thousand times. He kissed her and made his way down the length of her to be certain she was as ready for him as he was to be inside her. He let her guide him, watching her in the half-light of the full moon filtering in through an open curtain.

The phone rang. Jeremiah moaned and checked the clock, 3:35. "Nooo." The bed moved beside him and a smooth arm draped over his waist. "Henderson."

"Dr. Henderson, Lisette Harper is here. She's dilated and Macy says she's about ready."

"How's her blood pressure?" He left the warmth of bed and Junal for the cold wood floor and realized he was stark naked. He scrambled for underwear and socks.

"Seems a little on the high side, right now, but—hear that? That's Lisette screamin'."

"Dotty, I'll be there soon as possible." He hung up the phone and leaned over Junal's soft form. "If you have any desire *at all* to be my wife, you'll get used to this." He thought to kiss her on the cheek, but she turned and met his mouth for a sensuous, breathtaking moment.

She smiled and mumbled, "I'll see you later. If you'll call, I'll have your breakfast ready." She'd dozed off, by the time he made the door. He looked back, to be sure she was real. *If she's here when I return, I'll ask her properly.*

77

He pulled on his coat against the rain, as he left the front door, after bringing the dogs in from a few moments outside. He made a profound discovery; Daisy refused to pee in rain.

Chapter Nine

It was after 8:00 when Jeremiah stripped off his surgical gown. He took a moment to call. Junal answered his phone. "Hello there, beautiful." He found himself grinning.

Her voice was a soft purr, "Hello, lover."

"I'll be home shortly. I do believe the sun is shining." He stood at a window in the hospital.

"I'll make breakfast. See you soon."

They rang off and he made two more profound discoveries. He really missed female companionship and he missed having someone at home, waiting for him. It was time to make sure he landed the gorgeous Junal Finley, before she slipped away again.

He stopped by the florist shop, but they weren't open. He tapped on the window with a key until Myrtle Strickland opened the door with a frown.

"Dr. Henderson, we aren't open until 9."

"I can read, Myrtle. This is almost an emergency. Give me a lovely full bouquet about this big." He spread his hands apart a foot and a half. "Already in a vase, please."

She smiled. "Yes, sir. I can't charge you for it. The till isn't ready." She glanced around, until she found two arrangements with lots of color. "Give me two minutes." She took them to the back and worked her magic with the flowers, returning before the café doors, behind her, stopped swinging. "How's this?" She held up a garden full of brilliant flowers in one bunch.

"Fantastic. What do I owe you?"

"Twenty, but you can come by later." She waved him off.

He dropped a twenty and a ten on the counter. "Greatly appreciated, my dear." He balanced the vase carefully, and carried it to the car to prop in the floor with an atlas, two overdue library books and his black leather bag, all banking the perimeter. He made sure he could reach it, if he had to stop suddenly, and set off for the drive home.

The house smelled of frying bacon and baking biscuits, when he walked inside. He closed his eyes and thought about Saturday mornings, when he was a kid. Mama always put on a big spread for weekend breakfasts.

Junal rounded the corner in his flannel bathrobe. Her hair was still tousled from bed. She scooted across the floor in his wool socks. "Look at this, how lovely!" She took the vase from his hands and planted a kiss on his mouth. "Thank you." She set the bouquet on the table in the dining room.

He stood there, relishing the sight of her, in his clothes and his house. He knew he wore a stupid grin, but he couldn't help it. Slipping out of his raincoat, he never lost sight of her.

"I have to get back to the bacon, come on." She waved her hand to lead him further into his own home. "Boy or a girl? What did Lisette have?"

"A beautiful ten-pound boy." He rolled up his sleeves and poured a glass of orange juice, while she prepared his coffee. "He looks like he's three months old already."

"How many children do you want?" She smiled up at him, all the while tending breakfast.

"Children?" He still grinned.

"Do you want children?"

"Five." He stepped into her space and pulled her close to kiss her. When he let her go again, he missed the contact. "Will you marry me first?"

"Yes. I want four—kids that is. At least four."

He nodded and sipped his juice, all the while thinking how lucky he was, just to be in that room, with that woman, at that moment. "At least four."

After breakfast and a slow shared shower, he and Junal dressed for a walk. The dogs dashed out the front door, making for the meadow, as soon as the gate opened.

"Have you considered putting horses out here?" Junal's arm laced through Jeremiah's.

"I haven't had the time." He glanced down at her and measured his steps to her stride. "There were always horses out here, long as

I can remember, but they died off and I haven't replaced them. You want horses?"

"Yes, I love to ride."

"Done."

"What sort of wedding do you want?" He inhaled, still in shock at all that had transpired in twenty-four hours.

"A quick one will do." She smiled and watched his expression change.

"Why—why didn't you tell me you'd—not been with a man before?" He'd never been so shy of using direct, even blunt words.

"I did." She stopped, drawing him into a face-to-face confrontation, her hands resting on his shoulders, eyes peeking over the rim of her round sunglasses. "At Sally's? I said I'd waited for you all my life."

"I'm sorry, sweetheart." He cupped her jaw in his hand. "I didn't realize that meant everything."

Her face burned and she laid one hand over her heart. "Daddy always told me, all this was too precious to give away, except to the man I wanted to spend the rest of my life with. Yes, Miah, everything."

He tilted her chin to meet his eyes. "Your daddy was right, my love. I think a quick wedding is definitely in order. Courthouse?"

"I'm there on Tuesday and Thursday afternoons anyway, if you wanna meet me?" She turned her face to his hand, closed her eyes and kissed his palm.

The intimate gesture undid him. "It's a date. Give me a time and I'll be there."

"Two on Tuesday?" Her voice rose hopefully.

"After we have lunch together at one?" He moved in to kiss her mouth, as she nodded.

The phone beside the bed rang. Jeremiah rolled to his side and answered, his voice heavy with much needed sleep, "Henderson."

"You napping?" His mother sounded positively delighted.

"Yes ma'am. Junal and I are getting married, so you can go fetch Rose from Bobby's and come home." His bride-to-be propped in the doorway, fully dressed in jeans and smiling.

"Now why on earth do you think we had anything to do with you and Junal?" She covered the phone to chuckle, but he heard her anyway.

"I knew you were up to something wonderful. You forget; I know you." He sat up, keeping the corner of the sheet draped across his lap.

Junal rolled her eyes and left to pour his coffee.

"We'll be back in two days. You kids enjoy each other. Miah?"

"Yes ma'am?"

"You deserve her. Never think otherwise. The two of you were made to be together and—not speaking ill of the dead here, but you need to live and love and stop wasting time. Have the children you've always wanted, with the girl who always wanted you. You'll be surprised how different love can be."

He almost choked on emotion. "I just want what you had with Daddy."

"You're on your way, then. Have you set a date?"

"We'll go to the courthouse Tuesday to file paperwork, so the week after."

"No church wedding?"

"Maybe a reception here in the meadow? It's full of wild flowers. I can bush-hog a path into the field and cut an area to set up tables and such. Have to get Henry out to take a look and tune up the tractor. If it's rainy we can use the horse barn. Would that suit you and Rose?" He ran his hand through his graying hair.

"I'll call Deidra and order the cake. You can get Mary Ellen to handle the invitations but let her know today."

"I'll do that, after I check with the bride."

Junal handed over his cup of steaming coffee.

"Give her my love and congratulations."

"I'll do that, too. Bye, Mama."

Chapter Ten

"Can I reserve this booth?" Jeremiah addressed Sally. "Just Monday through Friday at about 12:45?"

"Well, you're always regular, so I reckon you can."

Junal walked in the door and saw Jeremiah sitting in the booth they'd used on Friday. She smiled, when he glanced up.

"Let's do that then, Sally. Unless I'm in surgery, my wife and I will be here. If we don't make it, I'll still pay you for lunch."

She waved her hand at him and turned away. "Pashaw!"

Junal tucked her skirt beneath her legs and slid into the booth. "What's this about booth rental?"

His voice was kept low. "Are you sure we can't get married sooner? I mean a week is a long time to have to wait, after our weekend together." He had no desire to share their secret with anyone.

She leaned over the table. "Whatever you want, Miah." Junal smiled sweetly.

"Let's walk over and get the paperwork done, if you have the time."

She glanced at her watch. "We'll have to make it quick. I have a meeting at 2:15."

"Alright then." He motioned the owner and called out, "Sally, we'll have the special and two teas please." He stacked the menus against the napkin holder. "Now, for the wedding. The courthouse will do to cement the contract, but have you thought about the reception out at the house, in the meadow, with family and a few friends? Mama's ordering a cake."

She laughed and clapped her hands. "Yes, splendid!"

"I'm glad you feel that way. She's leaving Ana's, running through Athens to fetch Rose and comin' home. I expect they'll be back tonight. So," He shrugged. "I guess you need to be home, eh?"

"It *would be* best to stay home." She smiled, a tiny dimple appearing in her left cheek, the cleft in her chin marking its perfection.

His heart melted. He sighed. "I know we have to wait until next week, but damn." He sat back when Sally appeared with their plates and the waitress behind her set their glasses on the table.

"Enjoy." Sally grinned and left them.

Jeremiah looked down at fried calf's liver, onions, gravy and rice with a side of greens. "Oh, I'm sorry. I didn't realize what the special was."

Junal smiled. "I love liver and onions." She cut the meat and scooped a forkful in her mouth. She chewed slowly and studied her beau try to get around touching the liver with his fork. She swallowed and said, "I gather you don't?"

He glanced up and smiled. "Nah, but I can live off love." He pushed the plate back and propped his chin in his palm to watch her.

Sally reappeared with a replacement hamburger steak. She slid the liver plate out and the steak plate in front of him. "I couldn't resist, you know. You're like a puppy dog after that girl." She reached for Junal's shoulder and squeezed. "We all feel like she's ours."

Junal eyes misted and she took a shaky breath. "Thanks, Sally."

***

Four o'clock in the morning Miah left bed for the bathroom. He paused when he opened the door, hearing the radiators pop, with the swish of hot water surging through them. The heart pine floor was frigid to his bare feet. He finished and stopped at the basin to wash his hands.

I'm missing a clue again. Damn, it was right in front of me and I swept it out of my way. Okay, go over recent conversations one more time.

By the time he reached his bed, it hit him. Agnes said they'd cut the timber off the Carson's place. Timber…that could be the key, especially if you're getting the land cheap, extended family, in a rush to sell, to take care of the estate, kids, taxes. He lay on his pillow and stared at the ceiling, awash in moonlight. Hell, the land would be a pittance, mostly hilly ravines, but the wood…that's where the money is. First cut might even pay for the original investment.

He turned on his side and swept his hand across the pillow Junal slept on for two nights. He pulled it close and buried his face in her scent. *God, I miss that woman.*

"Do you, Jeremiah Henderson take June Allison Findley, as your lawful wedded wife?" The Honorable Judge Ted Washburn turned his steady gaze on the doctor.

"I will." The doctor stood ramrod straight, a thousand thoughts banging around his mind, vying for attention.

"Do you, June Allison Findley take Jeremiah Henderson, as your lawful wedded husband?"

"I do, sir." She smiled sweetly, at her favorite judge, who agreed to marry them on his lunch hour.

"Then I pronounce you husband and wife. You may kiss your bride, Miah."

Jeremiah turned to his left and swept Junal into his arms, planting a big kiss on her lips. "Ah, that's more like it."

Ted Washburn chuckled. "Indeed!" His eyes took in a dozen of his staff who volunteered to be witnesses. "I'm pleased to introduce Dr. and Mrs. Jeremiah Henderson."

The couple hooked their arms together and walked through a short shower of confetti thrown by the Clerk of Circuit Court and the bailiff.

Junal grinned and applauded their efforts. "Thank y'all so much. You're each invited to the reception at the farm this weekend, Saturday at 3 pm. In lieu of gifts, please donate to the new hospital wing for newborns, under construction now." She had the same announcement printed on all the invitations, but felt the need to make sure that everyone realized she completely supported Marcia Henderson's commitment.

Jeremiah squeezed her hand and they left for their home, with their mothers in their wake. Miah dropped Margie off at Rose Findley's house, hopping out to fetch her overnight bag.

"Mamma, you don't have to do this, you know."

"I ken that, boy, but it's the polite thing to do. If you wanna run through the house naked, then do it!" She snatched her bag from her offspring and shooed him with the other hand. "I'm not decrepit. I can carry it myself. Now, go!"

Rose Findley stood on the sidewalk, blowing their children kisses. "I hope they have everything they ever want."

Margie joined her. "I wish them a load of trials, to strengthen their relationship and their characters."

Rose shot a frown toward her friend.

"Well, I do." Margie defended her statement. "Hell, nobody grows on Easy Street. We need conflict in our lives. Just pray it's never between them, but the world they have to fend off. And lots of grandchildren, Rosie, we want lots of grands to spoil and relive our youth through." Margie's eyes teared. She sniffed.

Rose wiped the tears coursing through her perfect makeup. "Here, here."

Margie stretched her arm across her friend's shoulder. "Let's go down to Athens and see that new Cary Grant movie. We can get a hotel. It's still warm; we can go swimming in their pool. What d'ya say, old gal?"

Rose laughed. "I don't know who you're callin' *old gal*. But, what I would love to do is go out dancing. There's a new nightclub, Bobby took me to, that hosts a jazz quartet on Tuesday nights. We could be there, when they open, and close 'em down. What d'ya say to that?"

"I'm in. Just let me take a powder room break and we'll paint the town of Athens tonight."

***

"Henderson." Jeremiah glanced at the clock, one eye closed to make out the number, through the haze of sleep. It was four in the morning. Junal stirred.

"Dr. Henderson? Isaiah Copeland here." The big man's voice was a mere whisper.

"What can I do for you, sir?" He glanced at his wife, curled on her side, looking sublime.

"Matilda aks me to call you and say our girl's in a bad way. Mattie thought she could bring this chil' into the worl' like she done all the others, but it jest won't come."

The doctor pulled on a shirt. "Where is she? At your house or hers?" He stepped into his jeans and yanked them up with one hand.

"We're at Ophelia's."

"I'll be there shortly. Tell Mattie to cross Ophelia's legs and tell her to try *not* to push."

"Yes, sir, I'll do tha'."

He kissed his wife's cheek and whispered, "I love you, Junal Henderson."

She squirmed and smiled, without opening her eyes. "Love you too."

With cold water splashed on his face and a comb run quickly through his hair, Jeremiah grabbed keys, passed Lester and Daisy stretched out on their beds, then headed to his car.

He parked in front of the plank house with a wide porch, where Ophelia and Daniel Walker lived. He jogged to the door, spurred on by the agony of a scream from inside. Isaiah Copeland had the door opened, by the time the doctor made the porch.

"Come on in." He closed the door securely. "She's jest in here." The tall long-legged black man led the way, through a curtain-covered doorway.

Ophelia Walker lay on a quilt, atop a cotton ticked mattress, sweating. "Thank God you're here." She looked exhausted.

"It'll be okay." Jeremiah spotted a basin of water on a side table and rolled up his sleeves. "How close are the contractions?"

He directed his question toward Mattie, who sat by her daughter's side, as he scrubbed his hands.

"One right after another, maybe a minute between, maybe none." Mattie's silky voice emanated calm in the room. She patted her daughter's hand.

The doctor's stethoscope searched for a heartbeat over Ophelia's swollen belly. "This is your first, isn't it?" He smiled at the dark eyed beauty, as another contraction struck.

She panted, until it passed, then squeezed out, "Yes, sir."

"Sometimes happens with the first birth, doesn't it Mattie?"

She grinned. "Shore does, if it's gonna happen atall, it's the first time." She massaged her daughter's hand and arm, brushed back her curls from her face.

"Ophelia, I want you to breathe in through your mouth, big gulping breaths." The doctor instructed.

She obeyed.

"Now let it out slowly through your nose. Focus on your breathing."

She obeyed again, as Jeremiah uncrossed her swollen ankles. "Okay, again. Mattie, you handle that end. I have this end covered. I'm making a snip to give him more room. It's easier to stitch and heal, if it's cut rather than torn." He perched on the end of the bed, made a two-inch incision, then waited for the baby's head to crown.

Jeremiah washed up in the basin, again, with a sidelong glance at the new baby and mother. He dried his hands on a large cotton flour sack, left beside the metal bowl.

Mattie met his eyes, with a smile. "I do appreciate you bailin' me out of trouble."

He grinned. "There's nothing more rewarding than this moment. Thank you for sharing it with me. I would have missed it, if you hadn't needed me." He unrolled his sleeves and snagged his bag. "You know the routine from this point, but if anything happens…anything bad…call me."

"Will do, Miah."

He turned to leave the ladies, then stopped. "Oh, and I'm supposin' you have your scales?"

"You supposin' correctly." Mattie smiled.

"Let me know how much he weighs. Junal and Mama'll both wanna know." The doctor passed into the front room.

Isaiah left the low chair he sat in and extended his hand. "What do I owe you, sir?"

"How 'bout a nice haunch of venison next time you kill a deer?"

The older man chuckled and looked at the floor. "Yes, sir, I can do that."

The front door opened and Daniel stepped inside, hoisting a metal lunch bucket. "I come as soon as they'd let me leave the plant."

Jeremiah extended his hand. "Daniel, you have a fine son, who's waitin' to meet you."

A grin spread on the new father's face. "Thank you for helpin' us out. What do I owe you, Doctor?"

"It's taken care of, son." Isaiah stuffed his hands into his overall's pockets.

"Get on in there." Jeremiah started for the door.

"By the by, Miah," Isaiah looked uncomfortable, in the low light of a single lamp.

"Yes, sir?"

"I don't know how to say this—but to say it. You be careful."

A chill ran up Jeremiah's spine. "Alright. If there's more to the warning, I'd be pleased to hear it." He dropped onto a sofa, draped in antimacassars.

Isaiah looked away. His voice lowered. "They's talk about some big outfit comin' in to take over the mountain. The sheriff has eyes and ears all over the place. Don't get in their way—tha's all I'm sayin'."

"You think I might be a problem?"

The older man grinned. "You a lot like yo' daddy in that respect. This thang's bigger than what we see."

Jeremiah nodded. "I don't even know what it is yet, Mr. Copeland."

"Isaiah, please, son. Your daddy told you we cousins, right?"

"Yes, sir, I am aware of our kinship."

The old man looked into the flare up of a bit of sap, in the kindling, he'd thrown on the fire. "My daddy and your grandmother was brother and sister." He met Jeremiah's eyes. "She could pass. Daddy was blacker'n midnight."

"Yes, sir, I remember them both, well."

"Might be best, you don't pursue this thing the Sheriff is mixed up in." He chewed his lower lip. "Take care and stop askin' questions. It would be best for Henry to quit snoopin' around too."

"I'll pass the word. By the way, Junal and I have a wedding reception. If y'all can make it out Saturday at 3, we're celebrating with family and friends. Let the kids know, too, please sir."

Isaiah nodded his head. "Will surely do, sir. Congratulations on your marriage. It's a lovely thing to be partnered with your best friend."

Miah grinned, "It certainly is."

Jeremiah cranked the Buick and sat listening to its' engine purr. How does Isaiah Copeland know what's going on with Henry and me? Then he remembered—he's the janitor at the courthouse. He's overheard conversations. This is bigger than I supposed.

Monday evening the doctor's phone rang in the study. "Henderson."

"It's Isaiah Copeland here."

He put down the paper in his hand and became alert. "Yes, sir?"

"First, Mattie said to tell you that our new grandson weighs 8 pounds and 10 ounces."

"A fine lad, that one."

"Yes, sir and they named him Ricardo Amos Jeremiah Walker. They callin' him Raj for short."

The doctor shook his head. "I'm honored. You tell your ladies I thoroughly enjoyed meetin' Raj and hope to see him soon, if they need me."

"There's somethin' else I wanna share wi' you. I overheard a discussion this mornin' at break. The sheriff and his brother-in-law was talkin' 'bout a *consortium* and someone called the Firemaker."

"It's a group called Firemaker," Miah half mumbled the words to himself.

"That's wha' they said." The older man agreed.

"Isaiah, don't get yourself caught eavesdroppin'."

The older man chuckled. "I'm one o' them invisible folk. White people ain't grown accustomed to actually seein' us darkies."

Miah's head dropped and he wondered if he was one of *those* white people. "Isaiah, I—

"Naw, you always have a howdy at hand, jest like yo' daddy."

"Thank you. You need to be cautious. People have died and I expect there'll be more corpses, as the stakes get bigger."
Whatever the stakes are.

"Yassir, I'll let you alone now."

"Goodbye, my friend." Miah laid the phone on the cradle and looked up to find his wife lounging in the doorway in a nightie that defied description.

"Aren't you coming to bed?" She watched her husband with a sleepy, sultry look that made his blood boil.

"Yes, ma'am. I was waitin' for you to fetch me." He rose and crossed the room toward her. "I was about to give up hope and come lookin' for you, when the phone rang."

"Another baby?" She glanced over her shoulder, leading him down the hallway.

"No ma'am, a message from a friend. And by the by, Mrs. Henderson, Ophelia's baby boy weighs 8 pounds, 10 ounces and he's named after me."

"You know when all those children named Jeremiah start school, they'll be confused every time their names are called."

"Come now, don't tease me." He turned her through their bedroom door and patted her tony bottom.

Chapter Eleven

Mary Ellen knocked on the door to room three and opened it. "When you finish here, you have a new patient in room four." She closed the door, after Jeremiah nodded.

He continued to stitch a deep cut on Mrs. Bonner's seven-year-old son's thigh. "We have to give you a shot too, Buddy. It's to keep you from being very sick." Next the doctor placed a large square of gauze over the stitches and wrapped the gauze around the bandage.

"Would I die if I didn't want the shot?" The red-haired, freckled-faced hellion grimaced.

Miah considered his question, while tying off the knot. "Yes, and it would be extremely painful to die from the disease you'd have, without it." He trimmed the suture thread and washed his hands. "If you're really good you'll get a sucker, if you aren't—well, we've never had to explore the possibilities of failure—yet." He stared down the defiant look on Buddy's face.

"I ain't scared of nothin'. I's just wonderin'." He scrubbed his forearm across his nose.

"Good, because it'll hurt a little bit. Knowing you're tough'll make it easier on your mother."

Mrs. Bonner observed with amusement.

"I'll send in a nurse with the shot." Miah started for the door.

"Hey! Ain't you gonna give it?" Buddy scrubbed his face with his grubby hand, drying away embarrassing tears.

"I have another patient to see. You'll be fine. Nurse Polly's nice, she won't make it any worse than it has to be." He began to close the door then opened it, peeking in. "By the way, stay outta the chicken coop and don't climb around on rusty tin. That's what got you into this mess. When the anesthesia wears off those stitches will hurt. *Don't touch 'em.*"

Buddy turned a reddening frown on his new nemesis. "You sure are bossy. Do you treat your help this bad?"

"Not all the time." Jeremiah winked at Mrs. Bonner and left the room. He shoved a thumb over his shoulder and nodded to Mary Ellen. "He's as ready as he's ever gonna be for a tetanus shot."

He knocked, then leaned into the door of room four. "Hello, I'm Dr. Henderson." He caught a glimpse of a very pregnant woman perched on the end of the examination table. He washed in the nearby sink and turned to face her, as he dried. "What can I do for you today?"

"I'm pregnant."

"I noticed that. First time?" He pulled the stool toward her with his foot and sat opposite.

"Yes, sir. Me and my old man moved down here from West Virginia, a week ago, and I set out to find a doctor to deliver our baby. After, I asked around at the diner, where we have breakfast, and made this appointment with you." She rubbed the side of her belly.

"West Virginia's a lovely place. What brings you to our neck of the woods?"

"It is unless you live near the mines, then…." She shrugged.

He looked at the chart for her name. "I see, Mrs. Dunhill. How far along are you now?"

"The doctor I saw at home said the young'un was due by first frost." She propped with her hands behind her back.

"There's a little difference in timing, as you're further south now, maybe the first hard freeze. Lie back and I'll fetch a nurse." He opened the door and stuck his head out. "Nurse, please."

Mining eh?

Mrs. Dunhill placed her feet in the cold steel stirrups. The nurse directed her to scoot her bottom down the table. She draped a white sheet over the patient and patted her knee. "I'll be right back." In moments she returned to the room with an array of metal instruments and the doctor in tow.

Miah examined Mrs. Dunhill, his mind racing to find questions he might ask that just sounded friendly, without raising suspicions. He couldn't think of a single one.

He stood, from the gray stool he'd perched on, and smiled. "I'll revise my estimation, Mrs. Dunhill. I believe you may be ready to deliver your child within six weeks."

She rubbed her belly and grinned. "Tha's good, Doc, really good. I can hardly wait for 'im to come."

"Shall we do a sonogram to see if it's a boy or girl?"

"No, I wanna be surprised." She sat up, with the nurse's help, and dropped her legs between the stirrups. "Thanks though."

"Is there anything else you need from me?"

She shook her head slowly, her hair slipping from the hasty bun she'd pulled it into fresh out of bed. "No sir, I can't think of anything right now."

"I'll see you back here in two weeks, then." He dried his wet hands, on a fresh towel, and dropped it into the laundry. "Should you need anything, before your appointment, give us a call."

Miah left the room, disappointed that he didn't peruse Mrs. Dunhill's chart before he opened the door. He might have come up with a reason to question their move to the area, that would have supplied more information.

Reception in the meadow

Margie Henderson studied her only son's frown. "Where's Junal?"

"She'll be out in a minute. She's waiting for Bobby to get here. He was picking up Rose on the way." He leaned to one side to see where Lester greeting a newcomer. "Think he's here. Lester's not kicking up a fuss.

"Lester loves everybody. Daisy's your watch dog." Margie sipped fizzy fruit punch, frothy with melting raspberry sherbet.

Jeremiah grinned. "She's a yapper for sure. Yep, here they come. Bob has a woman on each arm. Don't see anyone trailin', wanted to meet his wife." He left his mother to greet his bride, her brother and his mother-in-law. "'Bout time you showed up, old man." He extended his hand to Bob Finley.

Bob stood a few inches taller than the doctor and carried a bit more weight through his middle. He grasped the doctor's hand and pulled him into a hug. "God bless you, Miah for savin' my poor homely sister from old maidhood." He chuckled, but his humor lacked sincerity. Miah saw the sadness that lingered in Bob's eyes.

Junal looked exquisite in pale peach linen slacks, with a matching jacket. She donned flats and a wide brimmed silk hat for the occasion. Rose Finley, where Junal inherited her looks and taste, wore a similar coral ensemble, with the same results.

Jeremiah took Junal's arm and led the way to the open meadow and thirty or so guests who'd come to wish the couple well. Henry had mown the shape of a heart into the field of wildflowers and native grasses. A large canopy shaded the refreshments and a centerpiece floral arrangement. Chairs and tables were scattered around the area.

Margie stood to one side and watched the couple approach with satisfaction. No one in attendance could doubt her pleasure with the union.

Applause broke out amongst the attendees and smiles greeted the doctor and his bride. He reached for a glass of champagne, that his sister Carol poured and Joy passed around. Ana was prepared to cut the wedding cake, keeping the honey bees at bay, with a paper fan and a lace covered umbrella.

"To my bride, the most beautiful woman in the world, who loves me. I'm amazed every time she reaches for my hand. I could never imagine love like this could happen to me."

"Here, here," several voices rang out. Glasses clinked and the guests sipped their champagne or punch.

Junal smiled her perfect smile and raised her glass. "To my husband—finally!"

Laughter broke out and everyone drank to the doctor catching on to, what most of them had known for years. June Allison Finley held out for Jeremiah Henderson and no one else would do.

Henry stepped forward with a smile. "If I may propose a toast?" He perused the crowd expectantly.

"Let's hear it, Henry." Bobby Finley raised his cup of punch.

"To our favorite doctor and his charming bride, we all wish the best in the journey you've embarked upon, and can only hope, we each share your fortune, in matters of the heart. We'll rejoice every success and bemoan every disappointment, as your friends and family."

"Here, here! Well spoken, Henry." Bobby led the group, in drinking, to the couple.

Trixie, Henry's date for the occasion, leaned in close. "My goodness, sugar, that speech was a mouthful."

Henry met her puzzled frown. "I have many foibles, Trixie, but lacking eloquence is not one of them."

She brushed his arm with her breast. "I wanna learn all your fables, Henry."

His brows rose, a smile hinted at his amusement. "You are well on your way, darlin'." He patted her hand, that clutched his arm.

The Bailey Bluegrass Band struck up a tune, from their perch, on a temporary stage that Henry and Miah constructed from barn wood and concrete blocks. The banjo player stood in the center for a solo and guests clapped in time. Miah and Junal began the dance with a frolicking jig. Henry followed their lead, with Trixie, and Bobby led his mother to join the fray to whoops of encouragement.

"Do you think Bobby had a good time?" Junal's pale hair brushed Miah's arm as she laid facing her husband.

He shifted in the bed and rolled to meet her nose to nose. "I think he had a fine time. Everyone did, my love. Are you worried about him?"

"I always worry about him, Miah. There're moments, when he so full of darkness, that he's unreachable. Others, he's so jovial I feel like he'll burst." She smiled at her husband's crossed eyes. "You are too goofy sometimes."

"I just don't want you to be sad about your brother. Some things we have influence over, and can change, some we can't. If you insist, I'll approach him about having some tests run and see if—"

"No! He can't know I told you about his mood swings. He'd be very angry and we try to avoid offending him." She stroked Miah's face. "I love you, in case you don't know already."

He smiled and stole a brief kiss. "I love you, Mrs. Henderson. I may be remiss in reminding you, as we've been a tad busy this evening." He sobered and kissed her with longing.

Ana, Joy, Carol and Margie sat around the kitchen table, sipping cocoa spiked with spiced rum.

Margie reviewed each of her girls. "I hope all of you are happy with your brother's choice *this* time."

Carol swirled her nearly empty cup. "I certainly am. Junal's where he always should've been, if you ask me." She tipped the mug to her mouth.

Joy and Ana chimed in, "Amen!"

Joy giggled. "I'd give a nickel to look as good as she did, through an entire evening of dancing with every mother's son, who showed up."

Ana nodded. "She's a beauty for sure."

Margie shook her head. "Y'all talk like I'm in the company of cows, rather than four of the most gorgeous women, in the South. Need I remind any of you that you've all been homecoming queens and hold beauty titles in your own right?"

"No, Mama." Carol eyed her mother. "But it's not the same as just looking good all the time."

Miah's bedroom door opened and the group fell silent. The bathroom door closed.

"It's time for bed, girls. We'll resume this conversation in the morning." Margie stood.

"Are you going to relinquish your hold on the master bedroom, now that the right woman's in the house?" Joy pushed her chair, beneath the table, and glanced up at her mother.

"I'm moving out when I leave here tomorrow. I suggested, to Junal, that it would be wise to make the switch now, before she's expecting, as she'll need immediate proximity to the bathroom." Margie wore a satisfied smile. "It's not as though I'll never come back, but let me encourage all of you to get what you want to keep, from the house. It's Junal's now, and she has the right to do with it as she pleases."

"Yes, ma'am." Three voices responded in unison.

Chapter Twelve

Bobby's birthday party at the YMCA.

"Where's Bobby's wife?" Jeremiah had yet to meet his new sister-in-law.

"He said she had to work again, but this was too important to miss. She should have taken the whole day off." Junal sighed, looking miffed. "According to Bob, she's been working a lot of double shifts lately, says they can't keep reliable nurses at the hospital. I gave her plenty of notice, so she could mark the date, but obviously she didn't."

"Don't get yourself in a tizzy over it. Just relax and enjoy all your hard work. Maybe she'll come in when she's relieved." Jeremiah knew it wasn't likely. Hospitals tended not to accept late arrivers without prior clearance, but he had no idea that they were short staffed. He'd written referrals for several local candidates, who were told there was a waiting list, they'd be added to. The number of nurses in the area had recently increased, with the closing of several clinics and one hospital in rural areas.

Bobby regaled a group of men with a funny story. He couldn't keep the grin, off his face, and guffaws erupted. Several of his closest listeners, including Sheriff Little's brother-in-law, Bobby's boss, patted him on the back.

Ben Brennon walked in, with Trixie at his side.

Jeremiah caught a glimpse of the couple and leaned to Junal. "Did you invite Henry?"

"He said he'd promised his folks he'd take them to a reunion, up in Ashville, this weekend. Why?"

She looked the direction her husband focused. "Cheese and rice! That harpy is back with the jackass. Looks like Henry took the beating in vain."

Jeremiah watched the couple. "Appears she's nervous about it, maybe being found out that she's a two timer, huh?"

"Are you goin' to tell 'im?" Junal's hazel eyes widened.

"Not my place, unless he asks, then yeah, definitely." The doctor took a swig from the beer bottle he held.

The band tuned their instruments and tested microphones. The lead singer leaned into the nearest mic. "We wanna thank Junal and Rose for havin' us out tonight. Y'all come along and let's sing Happy Birthday to the guest of honor."

The crowd joined in the song, some louder than others, and honored Bobby Finley, who was in high spirits.

He took a bow and toasted the singers. "Y'all do a hell of a job for a bunch of drunks." He finished the last of his canned Coke and received a round of applause graciously.

Miah answered his phone, as Mary Ellen had left for home earlier, with a headache. "Doc Henderson, how can I help you?"

"Doc, It's Quinn. Headed home soon?"

"I can leave this minute. See you there." He grabbed his bag and left the office, at a lope.

The Deputy Sherrif pulled in the driveway five minutes after Miah arrived. He parked down at the barn, so his car couldn't be seen from the road. He walked back to the house and met Jeremiah on the porch.

"Come on inside, Quinn." Both dogs greeted them at the door, then shot outside for a run.

"Can I get you somethin' to drink? I'm having a glass of tea, how 'bout it? We'll sit in the kitchen."

The deputy nodded and followed. "Hated to call you at work, but somethin' has come to light. Wanted to see you, before your missus gets home." He glanced back at the front door.

The doctor poured tea and set the cold glasses on paper napkins, at the kitchen table.

They sat and caught their collective breath.

Doc spoke first, "Would this have anything to do with Bobby?" He crossed his legs, swinging his foot.

"Yes, sir. I haven't shared this with anybody." Quinn looked uncomfortable. "Might as well just say it. The sheriff is researching the files that you requested. Seeing if anything escaped his notice previously. He made a show of asking for them while I was in his office.

He mentioned Bobby Finley works at the muffler shop. Wanted to see if he was the mechanic on any of those vehicles, where folks were killed."

"Okay, I half expected that he would do that, when I heard he was upset that I'd taken the files." Jeremiah studied the ceiling fan. "If he has Bobby's work schedule, I could see him trying to tie Bobby's mental issues to the deaths. I'm sure the sheriff's brother-in-law would be happy to give him the information. I also think Bobby'd make a great fall guy." He turned his searching eyes back to the deputy.

Quinn sighed heavily. "Yeah, it's lookin' that way. Just be prepared, is all I'm sayin'. On the other matter, trying to buy up the land off the next of kin, of said victims, sheriff is making headway. He's had one family, 'bout two miles up, who wanna sell. Kids are all grown and gone. Jacksons moved in about 15 years ago. Older couple, first case of poisoning. Mister restored an old car, bodywork was his hobby. But come time for mechanical work, he took it into pros."

"On a day when Bobby was working?"

"Looks that way. Also, keep in mind, the schedule records can be made to show what the manager wants it to show. Unless Bobby was in jail or the hospital, he can't dispute it." Quinn took a big drink of sweet tea.

"We need to find out why the sheriff wants to buy the land he's after. Is it coal?"

"I've never heard of coal, up here. Primary mining efforts in Georgia are marble, gold and other precious metals and stones."

"Coal came to mind, because a new patient has moved down from West Virginia and her husband mined coal."

Quinn looked pensive. "Might have to do with preparation, get the mining business set up. People are trained for that one job. It would require a professional, to set up for open-pit mining."

Jeremiah jumped to his feet and yelled, "I know what it is, Quinn. Why didn't I think of it before? Damn!"

"Wanna share what you're goin' on about?" The deputy asked, smiling.

"It's copper, my friend. We're on the southern side of The Copper Basin. Because all this land is privately owned, on *this side of this* mountain, it hasn't been mined. All of it is in farming and timber. Until some slick entrepreneur comes along, with *plenty* of cash, they

can't touch the copper veins here." He sat again and chugged his tea, then said, "There's a rock, out by the horse barn. It's an igneous rock. It's always been there, too big to move and is probably the top of a boulder. Daddy showed me a vein, tiny— nothing huge, but the teller is the *kind* of rock that copper veins run through. It's a softer rock, easier to mine. They use an open-pit mining system."

Quinn sat back in his chair and nodded. "I get it. It ain't gold, but…"

"That's right! It's a sure thing and it isn't *always* blasted out of the ground. The landscape takes a beating and in two generations, the scars scab over. But think about this era we live in. All the wiring, electronics, plumbing pipe, on and on, needs copper. It's worth a bundle, should there be as much, on this mountain, as has been dug out in other parts of the Basin. Ratchet Mountain was formed, by the same volcanic action, as the rest of the Appalachians."

The deputy spoke up, "I don't want to live in a slag pit, Miah. How will folks up here take to mining goin' on around them?"

"They're not wanting to live in a slag pit either. They want life to continue on the way, it's always been, the past hundred years." He scrubbed his bristly chin. "I'll do a bit more research and see if the odds are in our favor or if we're doomed to become a mining operation. The reason the Basin hasn't been extended this far south is the stronghold of the families. I'm third generation, hoping to create the fourth generation of Hendersons on this mountain. I'm not giving in or giving up—no matter what." He sat back in his chair. "You be careful, son. Don't endanger yourself or your family."

"Yes, sir. I'm goin' to my house directly to see if my son mowed the yard today, like I asked him to. He's 12, you remember bein' 12?" He stood.

Miah joined him. "I'd rather been fishing than mucking horse stalls and mowing the grass. Loved ridin' the tractor, though. Tell me, before you go, do you have any good horse stock? Junal wants horses." They walked to the door and onto the porch.

Quinn looked out at the horse barn. "Is your barn in good shape?"

"It is. I had everything cleaned out after the last horse succumbed to old age. Mamma said he was 52 years old. There's room for at least five full grown horses." They stood in the yard, pondering the barn.

"Let's meet up Saturday at my place. You can look over the stock. It would be a good thing to get bonded horses. I have two fillies, from the same mare. Sweet girls. Bring Junal and let her try 'em out. She'll know what she wants." Quinn opened his car door.

Miah said, "About two o'clock?"

"Yes sir, that works." The deputy climbed into his car and waved as he passed the doctor.

Chapter Thirteen

Mary Ellen tapped on the office door before ducking inside. Jeremiah glanced up.

"Your mother-in-law is on the phone." His secretary crossed her arms, giving no indication she was leaving him to privacy.

He reached for the set and pressed a square button that blinked on hold. "Rose?"

"Miah, I hate to bother you at work but—"

"Nonsense, I'm always available to you. What's wrong?" He stood, listening closely.

"It's Bobby." She stifled a sob and continued, "He's in jail in Athens. His wife accused him of beating her. Miah, that's just not my son."

"I see. Give me a second, Rose." He covered the mouthpiece and met Mary Ellen's gaze. "Clear my calendar. Urgent appointments can be shifted to another doctor or Polly can see them."

His secretary nodded and left to complete his unusual request.

He gathered his black bag. "Rose, I'll pick you up in five minutes. Have you called Junal?"

"Yes, she's parking her car, out front now. She told me to call you at once, so I did."

"I'm on my way." Jeremiah laid the set in the cradle and grabbed his hat.

***

The doctor sat across a worn table scarred with graffiti and etchings. A hefty guard led Bob Finley into the tiny room, his hand tightly gripping the handcuffed prisoner's hefty upper arm.

Miah watched and nodded acknowledgement, as the guard stepped away. "Bob?"

His brother-in-law lifted a hooded gaze to the doctor's. His right eye was swollen and blackened from a recent thrashing.

"Bobby, what happened?" Miah leaned close to his friend.

"My wife found another loser she likes better than the one she married."

"Has this been going on for a while?"

Silence settled, until Bob sighed. "Most likely." He turned his head and checked the guard's position. "Told me last night, when she came home to pack. I followed her out and he, the boyfriend, jumped me from behind. I think I won the fistfight, but the war's lost for good." He studied the table, full of the history of every man and woman who'd used that spot to unload their burden of misery.

The doctor spoke softly, "I'm gonna get you outta here, man."

"Miah, don't. I'm a total waste of time and resources." His puffy cheek was wet from tears.

"You're my friend and the brother of my beloved wife. I'd take a bullet for you. Time and resources are just a beginning, Bobby. Now, try and be specific about what happened. Junal will handle the legal end, but I don't want her to see you this way."

The prisoner sighed again and attempted to pull his wrists apart, impeded by the metal cuffs. He growled in frustration. "I can't bear confinement! I'd rather be dead!" He glanced back at the guard, who took a step toward him.

Jeremiah reached across the table.

The guard approached. "No touching the prisoner, Dr. Henderson."

Miah withdrew his hand. "Sorry." He patted the table. "Just a little longer, Bob. Give me an hour and we'll have you sprung. Can you do that?" He locked eyes with his friend.

Bobby Finley nodded, his voice low, "Yeah, sure, Miah."

***

Jeremiah handed his checkbook to Junal. "Go post bail for Bobby. I have a call or two to make. I wanna get him into rehab."

Her large hazel eyes dripped. "Miah, we can't take your money." She laid the checkbook against her husband's chest. "It just isn't right for you to be spending—"

"Junal, he's my brother too, and the only reason I'm able to stand here today, is because he caught a leg full of shrapnel." He gently grasped her wrist. "Now, go, girl."

Her shoulders drooped, but she left him, her heels clacking on the concrete floor as she walked away.

"VA won't do anything to help." Rose gripped her handbag close. "We've tried to get him in before, but there's always a big waiting list."

"There's a private clinic in Atlanta. I have a connection there."

"Miah, we can't afford—"

"Rose, let me do this." The doctor dropped into a squat, in front of her chair, to look into his mother-in-law's eyes. "Please allow me to do what I can. Your family is mine too, now. When I asked Junal to marry me, I knew what I was steppin' into with Bob. I owe him my life. If he hadn't been in the middle of the shelling that fateful day, I would have died. I wanna take care of him."

She met his eyes, the corners of her mouth turned down, her chin quivering. "Okay, son. Thank you."

The doctor stood in time for his wife's return, to the waiting room.

Junal plopped onto the patched vinyl covered sofa. She carefully dabbed her eyes with a hankie and rolled her gaze toward her husband. "I don't know how to thank you for doin' all this, Miah."

He dropped down beside her and draped his arm over her shoulders. "We're in it together, wife."

She laid her head on his shoulder. "You don't know how comforting that one word is to me. I love being your wife. I long for the day the drama dies down and we can just be excited with the prospect of a child."

"We'll never be bored, sugar." He kissed her forehead. "I need to make those calls." He left the ladies and headed downstairs to a phone booth.

***

Junal met Miah for lunch, sliding into their booth. She whispered, "Wanna know a secret?"

Married for 90 days, Miah expected a 3 month celebration. "Of course, I do!"

He reached across the table and held her hand.

She whispered, "Do you prefer Daddy to Pa or Pop?"

He looked confused for 30 seconds. "What?"

She nodded, grinning. "There will be a noisy addition to our quiet, country lives."

Miah asked, "We're getting another dog?"

She slapped his hand. "You! I don't want to tell anyone else, just yet."

118

"Fine with me. Who did you go to, the new obstetrician?"

"I did, just wanted to be sure, before I told you." Her smile widen.

Chapter Fourteen

Two months later, after rehab

Bobby ran his hand over his face. "I never meant for this to happen, Junal. *Please* believe me."

She cocked her head to one side and studied her brother. Her voice softly purred, "Bobby, I believe you, because I want to. Our current situation is, you have to admit, a bit precarious." She held her head high and crossed her arms to ward off the chill, of the old mining shack. "Look, why don't we go the back way and down the mountain. You know how to get out of here." She dug into her purse. "I brought you money to start over." She produced a roll of $50 bills and stuffed them in his shirt pocket.

Rustling leaves, behind the remnant of the building, pulled Bobby back to the present. He raised his rifle. "Who's there?"

Henry kept his voice low. "Henry Phipps, Bob. Can I come in?"

"What the hell are you doin' here, Phipps?" Bobby turned his back to Junal, to peek out the opening left by a cross-hatched door that lay half hung by one hinge.

"I need to talk to you, pal." Henry neared, hands aloft. He stepped slowly, so as not to alarm his friend. "I wanna let you know what's happenin' on the summit." He slipped his slight frame through the gash and carefully picked his way through rubble. He took a long look around, afforded by the rising sun. "Man, I haven't been in this place in years. The last time we came up here was before you left for Nam. Remember that?" He tried a toothy smile on his exhausted, frazzled friend. "Got caught in a hell of a storm, when we were fishin' down in that burn." He pointed to the valley below and glanced past Bobby, to his sister. "Mrs. Henderson, how you doin'?"

She tried to smile. "Fine, Henry. How's my husband?"

"Fit to be damn tied." He watched Bobby peripherally. "He's threatened Sheriff Little with everythin' short of a firin' squad." He stuffed his hands in his jeans pockets and turned back to Bobby. "They've got snipers out there, buddyro. You know what that means?"

Bobby nodded his head. "Yeah, suicide by cops." He glanced at the opening of the cave, mumbling, "Wonder if there's still ghosts in this place."

"Most likely. They're no match for you, though. " Henry offered Bobby his hand. "You get outta here. I'll take Junal back, as soon as you've had enough time to make it through the cavern tunnels."

Bobby smiled. "You remember that? Hell, they may be collapsed by now, Henry, that was a lifetime ago."

"But maybe it's still passable. If you make it through—take off." He pulled out his wallet slowly. "I brought you all the cash I had, but it's no small sum. A thousand dollars should get you to Mexico and find you a place. Then all you have to do is write—"

"We can keep you supplied, until you get settled, Bobby." Junal chimed in, "Henry's right, all you'll need is a post office box and we can still be in touch. You already know about the Vietnam veterans' group, in Mexico, who can help you find yourself."

He nodded. "Junal, Little and his crew aren't goin' to stop huntin' me, just because I escaped the trap they set last night. Me and Henry can't be the only ones, who know about the cavern and where the tunnels lead."

"Look, Henry will stay here and pretend to be you, until you have time to get clear. Just go—at least *try* to escape." Her lovely hands tightened into fists. "The longer you wait, the more likely it is, that someone, who knows the mine, will wander up and volunteer to head you off. Now, go." She pointed to the dark yawning mouth of the cavern.

Bobby looked at her again. "I didn't mean for any of this to happen."

"I know. Forget the plans you had comin' up here. It's time to run."

"Forgive me." He hoisted his backpack and slung the rifle across his shoulders. "You got the truck keys?" He asked, as he turned to the opening.

"Of course, I do, you big lout." She hissed, "Now, go!"

He ducked through and switched on his flashlight, shuffling down the passage. Soon, his light was too far away to be seen, his steps too distant to hear.

Junal wiped her face, smearing dirt across her cheek. She studied Henry for a moment. He intently listened to something far away, saying goodbye to his friend again. "Henry?"

He glanced her way. "Yes ma'am?"

"How likely is it, that you and I can get outta here without gettin' shot?"

"Not very, I'm sorry to say. I overheard Little tell his men to shoot to kill. Doc blew a gasket and threatened to call the state boys in. If he's done that, and they get here in time, we have a chance of walkin' out, but if Little's still in charge…." He shrugged.

"You didn't tell Miah you were coming up here?"

"No ma'am. He'd have wanted to come and it's too dangerous. You have to know this place to walk around without bein' seen. I been within spittin' distance for half an hour. Doc's not enlightened." Henry grinned and glanced down at Junal's swollen belly. "I know you're tired, but we need to give Bob time to get past whatever rubble pile he runs into, in there. I don't want them bringin' in hounds and findin' him before he makes the highway."

"What highway?" She tried to maintain a modicum of decorum.

"Can't tell you that. They have ways of makin' you talk. They can't get squat outta me." He walked to the entrance of the cave.

123

Eyes closed, he listened. After a moment he placed his hand on the rock. "Godspeed, brother." He looked around. "We need a white flag."

Junal stood, from her perch, on a broken bench, with a sigh. "Turn around." She hiked her tent dress, as soon as the mechanic presented his back to her, and stripped off her half-slip. "Okay." She held out the delicate fabric. "Be careful. It's part of a matched set."

Henry made a grab for the slip, smiling. "Now, why didn't I know you'd come prepared?"

After more than an hour passed, Henry hoisted the white flag, that he'd fashioned from Junal's slip and an old termite ridden board. "You need to stay behind me. They'll see it's not Bobby, but that doesn't mean there isn't someone out there, who dislikes me, and would use this opportunity. I'd hate to mess up that pretty ensemble by accidentally spattering my brain on it." He reached through the opening and prayed someone sane saw the white flag. He moved slowly, as nimble as a cat.

Junal stayed behind, trying not to crowd Henry. She picked her way through the debris, doing her best to not cry. There would be time for tears later. They had to extricate themselves first. "Henry, do you think he's through?"

"Yep, the last run I did down the tunnel, the way looked clear. I think he's probably flagged a semi by now, on his way to Mexico. Checked for ghosts, but there were none *visible*." He took another step, the hair on the back of his neck, stood rigid. He flailed one hand behind him. "Get down!" He dropped to a squat, with Junal following.

She whispered, "What is it?"

Henry scanned the ridge. A glint appeared halfway up the mountain on the other side of the narrow valley. "Right up yonder, someone's takin' a peek at us, through a high-powered scope or binoculars. Just wanna be sure they see it's us and see the flag."

"Please don't get my slip shot up, Henry." She smiled when he turned to frown at her.

"I'll do my best. Okay, let's keep our hands held high and try to move a little ways." He hoisted his hands and Junal did the same.

Henry's shout echoed through the ravines and hollers, "Hey-oh! Hey-oh! We come in peace." He threw a remark over his shoulder. "I've always wanted to say that."

Junal giggled, a frantic sound. "I just wanna to see my husband."

Henry shouted again. "Hey-oh! Hey-oh!" He spoke to Junal again. "Surely they've seen us by now."

A shot rang out, echoing through the hills and hollers.

Junal skinned her knee and twisted her ankle when she fell. She pushed herself up, scanning the area. Henry lay prone, his face turned away. "Henry? Henry?"

No movement.

Junal crawled to reach him. A puddle of blood formed where his face met the ground. "Oh, Henry, please don't die. Somebody's got to get me outta here." She pulled herself along another few inches and tried to turn his head. "Henry?"

He groaned, then sighed, mumbling against the rock he rested against, "God in heaven what just happened? Junal?"

"I'm right here, Henry. I think you're shot, but I'm scared to raise up to see. There's blood beneath your face."

He lifted his head and turned it slowly toward the doctor's wife. "Are you hurt?" His eyes remained closed.

"No." She reached for the crease in his forehead. "Looks like a flesh wound, but may be deep. Can you open your eyes?"

The mechanic tried, stretching his face muscles to keep them open. "Just wanna sleep." His eyes closed again.

"Henry, it's a long way down this mountain and I can't go alone. You're gonna have to wake up and help me." She sniffed, trying to stifle the tears.

"Yes, ma'am." He attempted to push himself upright. Another shot rang out, striking a boulder just beyond them. He dropped to his former position. "I'm no brain surgeon, but believe it's past time to get outta the line of fire." He rolled and crawled through the mouth of the cave.

Junal followed on her knees.

The two of them inched through the gut of the cavern, dodging stalactites. The floor of the cavern was damp and cold. A tall, vague white shape appeared in a corner. The flashlight's glow

126

made it seem to move. Junal grabbed the back of Henry's shirt. "Henry, need your light cast over there." She pointed to the corner.

He turned and quickly flashed a beam in the direction she pointed. "Just the humidity." He assured her.

Henry heard running water. "Let's take a turn up ahead, I think to the right, we'll find the source of that water I'm hearing. Be cautious where and how you step."

He took the path first, holding his light low, to point out the pitfalls.

Junal took tiny steps, trying to slide her feet across the wet floor. The thought of a cool drink of water encouraged her hope. At least inside the cave, there were no bullets flying.

Henry handed her the flashlight. "Let me be sure it's alright. Looks fine, nothin' dead in it, or around it, that I can see." He knelt and scooped up a handful of icy water and sniffed, then tilted it into his mouth and nodded. "Come on, get a drink and we'll rest here for a few minutes." He stepped to the side and held the light for Junal.

She followed his method and purred at the feeling of the water in her mouth. She swallowed a few handfuls and splashed her face. "Feel like I might live through this, now."

She stood, with Henry's help, and they continued on their journey.

After a quiet twenty minutes, Henry paused. He shushed Junal and pointed to his ear. He indicated, through sign, that he could hear movement ahead. They stepped away from the path and took cover behind a large boulder. Five minutes later, two men were heard whispering to each other, as they picked their way through the cave from the opposite entrance.

Junal whispered to Henry, "That's Miah and if I'm not mistaken, Quinn McAdams." She moved to stand up, with Henry's help. "Miah?"

The doctor shone his flashlight on her grubby face and hurried forward. "Oh, thank God, Junal!" He wrapped his arms around her. "Are you hurt?"

"Just my ankle. Henry was shot, grazed his head."

Her husband opened his black bag and tended her twisted ankle, wrapping it snuggly. "Henry, you're next. Get over here." He had Junal hold the flashlight and cleaned the bloody crease on the mechanic's forehead. "It's a groove that'll leave a scar, but it stopped bleeding. I sent Quinn back. He doesn't need to be seen here. Henry, you know how to get out of here and down the mountain?"

"Yes, sir."

"Bob's gone?" The doctor asked.

"Yes, sir." Henry answered.

Miah turned to Junal, "See any ghosts?"

Her mouth opened, she looked at Henry.

Henry said, "No sir."

Jermiah smiled, "Good man!" He repacked the satchel and stood. "Let's go home." He offered his wife's his arm and helped her walk a little faster, to the source of light, near the end of the cavern.

Henry climbed into his shiny pickup and left, waving as he passed Bobby's truck.

Once inside the truck, Miah asked, "You want to tell me why you came up here with your brother?"

They sat in silence for a minute, before Junal found words. "He was going up to the mine shack to kill himself." She sniffled, her voice shaking, "He didn't want it to be a chore for us to clean up. He asked me to ride with him, and take his truck home." She broke into a sob.

Miah held her hand and found his hankie to clean up the tears.

She continued, "He wanted me to take the truck, because we'll need it with the horses. I stayed with him, for the climb, to see if I could talk him out of killing himself. I'd cleaned out my savings account and gave him the money. Told him to run, put all the distance he could between here and Mexico." She blew her nose on a tissue and continued, "There's a Vietnam vets organization there, that will help him. Then Henry showed up, with another wad of cash, and we talked him into going."

Her husband held her hand gently and soothed her with his silence. The quiet, early dusk of late fall settled around them.

"You did the right thing, sweetheart. I wish I'd been here to say goodbye to him. Anyway, maybe when you hear from him, we can meet again. This doesn't have to be forever."

Jubal leaned her head against Miah's shoulder. "Thank you for that hope, husband." She kissed him sweetly.

Chapter Fifteen

Finale

On Monday morning, Jeremiah walked into his office, distracted by the newspaper article he read. When he looked up, he met Mary Ellen's cautious look.

She tilted her head toward his office and whispered, "The State Attorney General awaits you."

The doctor grinned. "Good!" He opened the door and headed for his desk. "Glad you could take time to look into my query. First off, how you been, Marcus?" He reached across to grab the extended hand.

"Good, real good. Just had our third child, another boy. Em's doing well. Thinking we'll call it done, after this one. The other two are brawny lads, playing sports. How 'bout you, heard your wife passed and you remarried. Kind of sudden wasn't it?"

Miah'd nodded through Marcus' greeting. "It was a sudden thing to marry the girl I've always loved. She'd waited for me, to get through my foolishness." He crossed his legs and leaned back in his chair. "So, what brings you here?"

"Your sheriff brings me here."

Miah leaned forward. "How's that?"

"He a professional conman, Miah, slick as can be. Feds have numerous warrants for his arrest and I haven't figured out why there's not a picture of him in every Post Office in the country. They been trying to catch this rascal for 10 years. He slips away every time. Marshalls are handcuffing him right now. His wife gave us a chase, from the beauty parlor to their house. She ran inside and locked the doors. Last I heard, they cut her power and phone, but still talking to her."

"You have charges against her, as well?"

"She's his step-sister and the bookkeeper. If here is anything like the case in Montana, every business deal they make is a huge con. They start a company, in this case it's called Firemaker. They sell shares in a mining company and buy up land. Then, they vanish. On to the next place, same M.O. The land is never paid for, just contracted, with fantastic clauses full of promise, et cetera."

"I see." Miah pondered the few facts he'd learned. "How many other burgs has he bamboozled?"

"We know 12, maybe there's more, but if we can get him in a cell and keep him, there won't be another one. It'll be interesting to see what charges the Feds bring, but the way they talked, the crew *will* be considered flight risks."

"Does this include the muffler shop in Athens?"

"That business is now closed and the owner is charged with 5 counts of manslaughter. We're still trying to suss out the first 3." Marcus spread his hands. "It'll take some time."

He stood and leaned on the back of the chair. "Give Miss Junal my regards. Someday, we'll get together. Ya'll come on down to Atlanta and see us."

Miah walked his friend out. "We'll do that. Ya'll are welcome to come up and bring your boys. We're restocking the stable. Bought 2 fillies last week."

"Yeah, I miss this place sometimes. The city wears me out." Marcus turned and the two men shook hands.

"Be seein' ya. And thanks again for looking into this mess."

"No problem. Bye, Mary Ellen."

"Goodbye, Marcus." She called right before the door closed. She turned to Miah. "Is he taking out the bad guys?"

"It's in process. Feds are in town as well. This thing became far more complicated than we knew. I'm glad it didn't go any further. Many patients today?"

Mary Ellen looked down the appointment book. "Only three this morning. Nothing this afternoon—yet."

He nodded, "Think I'll take this afternoon off. Need to see to new tack for the horses."

"Is Junal thrilled?" His secretary asked.

"She is, but can only ride at a walk, right now. Baby is progressing." He smiled and returned to his office.

Five months later

Junal Henderson opened her eyes, from her brief nap, to see her husband beside her bed, in a chair. He had a blanketed bundle in his hands. He gazed lovingly.

"Is he beautiful?" Junal asked. "I didn't get to see his face."

Miah shifted and turned the sleeping bundle toward his wife. "He's perfect and he's a handsome lad." He shifted his son to rest in his left arm and reached for his wife's hand. "You feeling alright?"

She nodded. "Feel like I'm in a dream, Miah. Things are a little blurry, but the delivery went well, didn't it?"

He grinned. "Very smoothly. You were in surgery almost fifteen minutes. Probably why you feel fuzzy. I was waiting for you to hold him again for a few minutes, before the nurses make me give him back." He tucked the little bundle into his wife's arms. He stood over the bed admiring the two people he loved more than life itself. Tears coursed down his face.

Junal glanced up at him. "Please, don't start with recriminations. We've loved each other for a long time, Miah. But, I have to believe that we wouldn't be who we are, without the wait and heartache. We needed to be strengthened and that was our lot. Now, we're going to have the family, that I only dreamed

134

of building with you." She glanced down at their son. "And you, little mister, are going to be loved, loved, loved."

The door opened to the nurse. "Time for little bit to get weighed and measured. I'll bring him back soon."

Junal asked, as she passed her son to the nurse, "How about a name for the boy?"

Miah grinned. "It won't be Jeremiah."

Junal nodded. "I was thinking we'd use Finley as a middle name, a Southern tradition."

"How about Robert?"

Junal shook her head. "Bobby's first wife gave birth to a boy, who died 3 days later. Complications with his heart. He was Robert. How about David, after your dad?"

"David it is, then. David Finley Henderson. That's a mouthful. Suits him." He leaned toward her and grasped her hand. "Thank you! You're the best thing to, ever, happen to me, lady. And you just keep getting better. No recriminations."

They sat, in silence, until Davy was brought back for his momma to feed him. The doctor and his bride savored every moment.